# Awaken the Heart

Society of Swans
Book 1

## Penny Fairbanks

## ARE YOU SIGNED UP FOR DRAGONBLADE'S BLOG?

You'll get the latest news and information on exclusive giveaways, exclusive excerpts, coming releases, sales, free books, cover reveals and more.

Check out our complete list of authors, too!

No spam, no junk. That's a promise!

### Sign Up Here

www.dragonbladepublishing.com

*Dearest Reader;*

*Thank you for your support of a small press. At Dragonblade Publishing, we strive to bring you the highest quality Historical Romance from some of the best authors in the business. Without your support, there is no 'us', so we sincerely hope you adore these stories and find some new favorite authors along the way.*

*Happy Reading!*

*CEO, Dragonblade Publishing*

# CHAPTER ONE

*March 1811*

CAUTIOUSLY PEERING OVER the top of her book, Lydia glanced about the silent drawing room to find her family quite occupied—Mother with her embroidery, Father with his morning mail, and Edmund with the newspaper. The scene looked almost like a painting. Lydia slipped a floral bookmark between the pages and craned her neck toward the window.

What looked to be a mob of young ladies wrapped in soft spring colors, led patiently by a familiar dowager, approached Jenwick Park across the wide, immaculately trimmed lawn. Quiet excitement twinged in Lydia's heart, a small smile spreading across her otherwise impassive expression. Straightening her regal shoulders to an almost painful degree, she returned her attention to the drawing room, eyes skimming over the carved moulding, the rich tapestries spread across powder-blue walls, the fine furnishings—each element chosen with painstaking care to best display the family's wealthy taste.

"Mother, my friends have arrived. Might I go downstairs to meet with them?"

"Be mindful of your volume, Lydia." Mother sighed without looking up from her project, easing another blue stitch through the cloth. Lydia's eyes darted to her left, catching her younger brother's commiserating glance. Both she and Edmund knew

Lydia's volume had been fine. It was simply their mother's nature to find fault even in near perfection.

"Forgive me, Mother," Lydia whispered, lowering her head in deference. A brown curl tucked behind her ear slipped out. She brushed it away quickly before Mother could see.

"Yes, you may join them. But do not be too long. Remember we are hosting our farewell dinner. You have your new gown waiting for you in your dressing room upstairs, so you will need more time for minor adjustments."

"Certainly." Lydia nodded again. Despite her eagerness to see her friends, she kept her strides short and light as she crossed the ornately decorated drawing room, hands placed gracefully one on top of the other at her waist. Even for Lydia, Mother's constant criticisms grew tiresome. She had learned early on in her childhood that the best way to avoid them was to avoid any mistakes, no matter how minor.

"Enjoy yourself, sister!" Edmund called just as Lydia reached the door. She jumped at the unexpected noise and threw a glower over her shoulder before marching on. Her brother snickered and ducked behind his newspaper.

"Edmund! What did I just say about volume?" Mother's groan trailed down the stairs after Lydia, inspiring another faint smile.

"Ah, Miss Dailey. Visitors have arrived for you," the butler called as Lydia reached the bottom step, the front doors swung wide. He swept a graceful arm out across the grand foyer as six ladies streamed in.

"Do you really think?"

"Pure folly!

"I swear I had never heard something so—"

Voices overlapped, a babble of conversations clamoring in Lydia's ears. She normally detested noise, but now she welcomed it.

The butler cleared his throat. "May I present—"

Lydia suppressed the chuckle that sprang to her lips. "Thank you, Parkins, but that will not be necessary." She added under her breath, offering the older man a reassuring expression, "You know you need not make any formal announcements for this crowd when it is just me to hear it."

"Mrs. Dailey prefers it for any and all guests, no matter how well known to the household," Parkins whispered back, ridged nose in the air, ever Mother's most loyal servant.

As the butler completed his sacred task of announcing each of Lydia's lifelong friends, as well as Isabel's aunt and frequent chaperone, Lady Ainsworth, the women took their turns offering happy greetings.

"Dear Lydia, you must join us for a walk," Felicity announced, bright-brown eyes aglow as she bounced on her toes. "The day is perfect!"

Lydia narrowed her eyes at Viscount Eldmar's daughter. Isabel and Ellen exchanged glances that heavily implied their disagreement. "Is it? I thought it rather overcast when I looked out the window to find you all marching upon my home."

"It is perfect weather for those like my sister, who favor the chill for long walks," Mercy added, sending a bemused glance at Felicity, her twin, who wrinkled her nose in response.

"As long as one wears a shawl, the chill should not be much of a bother." Isabel wrapped hers tighter about her pastel-green walking dress that complemented emerald eyes.

"Come now, you will warm up quickly with the exercise," Clara, Ellen's sister as well as the youngest and cheeriest of the group, added. She held out a hand for Lydia, long, graceful fingers reaching out.

For the first time that day, Lydia allowed herself a proper smile—though she made sure her back was to Parkins, lest he report her minor indecency to Mother. She accepted Clara's hand and her friend linked their arms together.

"You see? I win! I knew she would join us!" Felicity boasted, the blonde curls framing her face bouncing with pride.

Quiet Ellen, standing right beside Felicity, started with a

squeak and stumbled back a few steps, only managing to stop herself before bumping into a vase half her size. She stumbled again when Felicity grasped her hand and yanked the shorter girl closer, slipping an arm around her waist.

Mercy, almost a perfect mirror of her sister, shook her head and looked about the foyer. "Was anyone else aware that we were competing?"

The young ladies all laughed, even Lydia. The rigidity of the Dailey family's typical morning slowly seeped from her muscles, relaxing ever so slightly. "Well, you have me now. Though I am not sure why you all did not wait until dinner. You will be here again in just a few hours."

Clara sighed and patted Lydia's hand where it rested on her forearm. "We must enjoy one last walk about Bainbridge before we leave for London, just us. Our attention will be too divided during the dinner party. Mrs. Dailey always spreads us out around the table."

Lydia shifted her hand to squeeze Clara's. "Only so you do not cause any ruckus and disturb the peace of Mother's distinguished guests." She chuckled before returning her attention to the other woman lingering in the foyer. "Will you be joining us, Lady Ainsworth?"

The older woman, who had been watching the friends' merry conversation with a contented smile, waved a gloved hand that perfectly matched her plum dress. "No, no, I thought I would stay here a while and pay a visit to Mr. and Mrs. Dailey while you ladies enjoy your walk. But do stay on the grounds and come fetch me when you are ready to venture further."

"Mother and Father will be so pleased to see you," Lydia called over her shoulder, struggling to keep up with Clara, who pulled her toward the door. "Wait, my bonnet!" she cried.

A hand shot out from some hidden corner, offering a blue bonnet trimmed with white flowers. The maid curtseyed as Lydia accepted with gratitude. Thanks to Mother's rigorous standards, their staff had come to learn how to anticipate the family's needs.

It would have been alarming if it were not so wonderfully useful.

The ladies settled themselves into pairs, Lydia with Clara, Felicity with Isabel, and Ellen with Mercy. Patiently waiting footmen threw open the double doors once more for the six friends, a cool breeze snapping at their bright faces.

Leading as she often did, Lydia glided down the front steps, onto the lawn, and around the corner of her generously sized home. "What news do my companions bring me since our last meeting?" she asked, raising her voice over the whistle of the early spring wind. The pairs spread out in a long line, side by side, looking straight ahead at the faint glimmer of Jenwick Park's lake in the distance.

"Since two days ago, you mean?" Isabel replied with a light laugh.

"Certainly." Lydia nodded sharply. "When we are used to seeing each other every day, I expect to be bombarded with news after any longer absences."

Each lady offered the details of their comings and goings about Bainbridge and the surrounding area, from luncheons to carriage rides to card parties to visits from far-flung family members. The waning of their country days always necessitated overwhelming schedules to see everyone off before the mad rush of the London Season. Laughter and exclamations floated into the gray sky. It seemed a little brighter at least, as if responding to her friends' lively banter.

When they reached the lake, the pairs broke apart and settled onto the comfortable benches at the edge of the calm, silvery water.

"Can you believe another Season is already upon us?" Clara asked with a sigh, scooting closer to Isabel. The latter unfurled her handsome yellow shawl of muslin and draped it over the younger lady's shoulders, then did the same on the other side for Ellen.

Felicity, seated beside Lydia on the other bench, leaned back with a groan in a rather unladylike fashion. Lydia arched a brow at her friend. When that did not deliver her message, she gently tapped Felicity's leg with the back of her hand. Felicity groaned again and scooted away, a teasing glint in her dark eyes, without correcting her posture.

"Our mother is driving us mad with all her plans for the upcoming Season. She has our entire first week scheduled already," Felicity explained. The girls offered a chorus of understanding mumbles.

"I swear, she has had the poor maids and footmen unpack everything and then pack it all again three times now," Felicity continued, building speed, her hands gesturing through the air. "And for some daft reason, she decided just yesterday that she wants the downstairs sitting room—the one no one ever uses— rearranged. Just before we leave for months! Not to mention all the new dresses she has fitted us for. It seems like quite a waste to me when our dresses from last Season were only worn once or twice each."

Lydia nodded in agreement, folding her hands in her lap. "Our mothers have that in common. Mine is going to every length possible to send me down the aisle—finally. Still, we should be grateful to have mothers who care about our futures…even if it does seem rather excessive at times."

"I hope that everyone will have enjoyable Seasons this year," Ellen offered slowly, her gentle voice almost swallowed by the ambient noises of nature. She leaned forward around Isabel and Clara to smile at the ladies on the other bench, quiet optimism alight in her lovely, blue eyes.

"Of course we will, dear Ellen," Mercy replied from Felicity's other side, her usually factual tone softening for the quietest and sweetest member of their group. "But I must say I agree with Felicity. The charm of Seasons wears away after being thrown back into the marriage mart four years in a row." The younger of the twins pursed her lips, her gaze growing hard as she stared out at the tranquil lake and the gently rising hill behind it.

"Besides, Mother does not actually care about our prospects

after our older siblings all married so well. She heard some whispers around Bainbridge that the fact Felicity and I remain unmarried at almost three-and-twenty is beginning to reflect poorly on her. And the viscountess cannot have that."

"Perhaps Lady Eldmar has been conspiring with my mother," Lydia added ruefully.

Isabel hummed, staring up into the cloudy sky. "Are the Reeve twins planning on starting their spinsterhoods early? And you, Lydia?"

Lifting her chin into the air—and surreptitiously glancing behind her at the dramatic silhouette of Jenwick Park rising up behind her—Lydia retorted, "While that is certainly not my intention, that seems to be the direction my path is taking. I have already turned three-and-twenty, after all. In the *ton*, that is considered an advanced age for an unmarried miss. They say a woman's life does not truly begin until she marries."

Felicity muffled a snort of derision, quickly shifting closer to the arm of the bench when she sensed Lydia's ire. Lydia stiffened and steeled herself to continue. "If spinsterhood is to be my fate, I shall accept it with grace. Though I cannot say the same for these two, especially Felicity," she added in a faux-whisper, eyeing her friends from the corner of her peripheral vision with a playful smirk.

"We should all consider taking the task more seriously this year," Isabel continued, "even if that means adjusting our expectations. That includes you, Clara." She leaned to the side and bumped the girl with her shoulder.

"Me? But I have only just had my first Season," Clara whined, pushing out her full bottom lip. She retracted it at Lydia's insistent cough.

Isabel chuckled and let her head rest against Clara's. "Yes, you. If you hope to have a comfortable future with a tolerable man."

"That is easy enough for you to say," Felicity grumbled to herself. In a flash she leaned forward and plucked up a smooth, round stone, turning it about with her fingertips, dirt clinging to white silk. "At least you have managed to earn a gentleman's interest. None of us have even had a proper courtship."

"Felicity," Lydia hissed, glaring at the lady to her right before glancing at the other bench. Isabel had gone rigid, her head lowered, leaving Lydia with no doubt that she had overheard.

"Forgive me, Isabel," Felicity offered, tossing the stone back to the ground with a soft thud. Her fiery eyes had turned remorseful. Though she could be reckless and temperamental at times, Felicity never aimed to be cruel. Lydia slipped a hand from her lap to grasp one of Felicity's, squeezing a silent assurance.

Isabel took in a long inhale and adopted a smile that none of the other girls fully believed. "Whatever happens is meant to happen," she quipped.

"Precisely," Ellen agreed, burrowing deeper under the shawl and closer to Isabel. She wrapped an arm around their friend's shoulder, one hand rubbing up and down Isabel's exposed arm. "Sometimes when one opportunity is lost, an ever better one reveals itself."

"Thank you, darling." Isabel sighed, shifting in her seat to curl into Ellen's comforting presence. Certainly not ladylike. Lydia held her tongue this time. Maintaining composure in the face of heartache was no easy feat.

"My sister is right," Clara announced, showering the group with her charming, bright smile complemented by rosy cheeks. "We should all be praying for each other's successes, wherever they may lead."

Catching Lydia's eye, Clara twitched her brows up and tilted her head expectantly. There was something so childishly earnest about the expression that Lydia could not help laughing.

"Very wisely said, my dear," she agreed with a sage nod. All the other girls turned to look at Lydia. She was the oldest of the group, if only by a few months. Her friends looked to her for guidance, and guidance they would have.

"Just as Clara said, and as Ellen said before her, we must

continue to be champions for each other," Lydia continued, sitting tall and poised. She had never sought the spotlight, yet Mother had taught her well how to manage when it chose her. And it would choose her if Mother had her way of marrying Lydia to a lord. "We have been champions for each other all our lives, no matter the circumstances. That is what we shall continue to do. And I do hope that at least one of us will graduate from the marriage mart with a happy ending this Season. Once one unlocks the secret, perhaps she would be so kind as to share it with the rest of us," she added with a chuckle.

As her friends echoed her sentiment, Lydia observed them each in turn. The Reeve twins, the Gardiner sisters, and Isabel Abbott—her dearest, most trusted friends. Each beautiful and fascinating in her own way, in ways they rarely recognized in themselves.

Here Lydia sat in the middle, easily the least compelling of the bunch. Why none of her friends had half the *ton*'s eligible gentlemen falling at their feet, she did not understand. For herself, she knew perfectly well.

A lump of emotion inched its way up her throat as the conversation shifted to lighter subjects, her eyes drifting down to the bed of rocks that disappeared under the lake's cool water. Her heart sank and settled in her stomach next to her silent, tenderly held dreams. While Felicity turned her nose up at such silly notions like love and Isabel regarded it as secondary to the practical necessities of life, Lydia aligned herself with the romantics of the group—quietly.

Nothing would have been more pitiful than to admit how ardently she longed for a gentleman's love...only to end up a spinster after all.

Looking her fifth Season in the face gave her no hope despite Ellen's and Clara's encouragement. The gentlemen she'd met always grew tired of her careful, reserved demeanor long before Lydia could even glimpse the sparks of a happy matrimony.

"Are you well, Lydia?" An almost imperceptible whisper to

her left broke through Lydia's shameful reverie. Her gaze snapped up, her personal admonishments shoved back down into the dark, where they belonged. Self-pity would get Lydia no closer to her dreams.

"Of course I am," she answered firmly, offering Mercy a flash of a smile.

The lady stared at Lydia, thoughts formulating behind her pensive eyes. Lydia nibbled the inside of her bottom lip, the only nervous habit she had been able to hide and thus protect from the scoldings of Mother and the governesses of the past. After another long moment, Mercy merely nodded, accepting Lydia's lie without believing it.

"If you had been unwell, I am sure our new arrival would change that," Mercy added in a whisper, glancing over her shoulder. Curious, Lydia turned.

"Sebastian." She sighed, relief rushing through her. The others noticed him striding across the lawn at the same time and waved him over. He reached one long arm up in response, dark coat unbuttoned and maroon cravat askew, a grin stretched over his face.

"I hope I am not interrupting one of your secret ladies' meetings," Sebastian called, his warm voice carried on the biting breeze. He bent low at the waist, arms spread wide, in a playful bow. Another gust swept his wavy, black hair away from his forehead as he righted himself, still smiling.

The girls laughed and welcomed him with smiles of their own. Sebastian Harrowsmith, another lifelong resident of Bainbridge, was almost as familiar to them as they were to each other. He took the last few steps and paused between the two benches.

"I am so very glad to see you all," Sebastian added. His eyes never left Lydia.

# CHAPTER TWO

THE FAMILIAR LIGHTHEARTED chatter of Bainbridge's most charming young ladies ebbed and flowed on the crisp breeze. No matter how many times Sebastian told them that the area's residents truly referred to them as such, they never believed him. The most charming of them all—at least in his humble opinion—walked by his side, her prim hand resting on his coat sleeve of gray wool.

Jenwick Park's vast lawn stretched before them, disappearing into a horizon of trees in the distance. Thin clouds above drifted across the silvery sun, temporarily casting the group in shadow. Coupled with the occasional surge of biting wind, winter still seemed the nearer reality than spring. Even stoic Lydia Dailey could not help shivering against Sebastian.

He tilted his head forward, trying to peer under the brim of her tastefully trimmed bonnet—done to perfection, as was her way. "Something weighs on your mind," Sebastian announced, mindful to keep his voice low so as not to draw the other girls' attention.

One thing he'd learned about Lydia during his years of growing up on the adjoining property, his parents' fond favorites and frequent guests of Mr. and Mrs. Dailey, was that she did not care for her true thoughts and feelings to be exposed to the outside world until the exact moment and manner of her choosing—which was oftentimes never, if she deemed that best.

"How do you know?" Lydia asked, peering up at him from beneath her bonnet with dark, inquisitive eyes.

Sebastian lifted a shoulder. "You are quiet."

The lady pursed her lips and lifted her nose into the air. "I am always quiet. Quiet is genteel."

Laughter erupted from the cluster of friends walking a few paces before them as Felicity just barely managed to complete a cartwheel, as if to emphasize Lydia's point.

"You are still."

This gave her pause. She narrowed her eyes at Sebastian, a silent command to continue. She must have truly wanted to know if she was focused on that and not on her friend's gratuitous breach of etiquette, especially with a gentleman present. Even if said gentleman had grown up beside them and considered them as good as sisters—or at the very least cousins of whom he was most fond.

Except for Lydia. The thought always jolted Sebastian. Because he'd spent the most time with her, given the closeness of their estates and their parents, his and Lydia's friendship had taken deeper root than the others. It was different in a way Sebastian had never dared approach aloud—most certainly not to her. Never, ever to her. Not if he wished to remain friends with Lydia and the other girls. He hardly allowed himself to approach it in the privacy of his own mind. Life was simpler when he managed to bottle that strange sensation, under the surface and out of the way. The morning's news had changed that.

"Usually, when we are out walking you like to look about. At the landscape, at our friends while they tell their stories and jokes."

Lydia looked straight ahead once more, steeling her gaze. Sebastian took the opportunity to smile. Goodness, how had his oldest friend also ended up the most stubborn? Still, he knew what it looked like when he'd broken through.

"If you must know, you nosy ninny, it is nothing you have not heard before. The usual worries of the impending Season. I fear my prayers for finding a match have grown repetitive in heaven's ears and in my own. I am not sure how much longer I can bear to repeat myself."

The words spilled out, still sharp around the edges despite the ache hidden within. Sebastian knew it well. His chest squeezed with pain to see her composed distress, her gloved fingers curled into a fist against his forearm.

It was his duty as Lydia's friend to do what he could to help. He had no desire to see this hurt ever again.

"I hope you receive these words with an open heart, dear Lydia," Sebastian started, keeping his voice steady despite the sudden churning in his stomach, "but perhaps it is time to allow yourself more enjoyment...more freedom. Manners are all well and good—believe me, I know what your mother would say— but it is also possible to be open and inviting at the same time. In that way, perhaps you will invite the right gentleman into your heart."

"Sebastian!" Lydia gasped, giving a scolding smack to his bicep in conjunction.

The five other ladies glanced over their shoulders and quickly returned to the lively poem recital performed by Clara. They had long since learned to leave Lydia and Sebastian to their own private world.

"Now is not the time to throw decorum to the wayside," she hissed under her breath. "And are you saying I am not inviting? Never mind that. You should be determined to take advantage of the next Season, too, Sebastian. You are to become baron after your uncle. Your family needs an heir. Bless the poor man for never having children of his own, but that cannot be your fate."

A knot tightened in Sebastian's throat. He straightened his shoulders as if bracing against the breeze, stretching his chest in the hopes of dislodging it. He had not wanted to come to this so soon. "I am afraid...."

"Sebastian?" Lydia nudged, concern creeping into her voice. Words did not often fail him.

"I am afraid we have received a letter on that very subject."

Lydia shook her head, a few loose curls at the nape of her neck dancing. "Do you mean to say….?"

"It appears that my uncle acted expeditiously after coming out of mourning for his late wife. So expeditiously, in fact, that he only just now wrote to inform us that he has acquired a youthful bride who will be delivering him a true heir in several months' time." Sebastian dragged every word past his dry lips.

"Dear Sebastian." Lydia gasped quietly, vibrant, blue eyes brimming with sympathy. "I am so very sorry. He had not informed you all beforehand that he would be remarrying?"

The weighty stone in his stomach sank even further. "No, he did not. He claims he wanted to surprise us with his miraculous news. I rather suspect he knew Mama would be beside herself at the thought that he would remarry so soon while she…."

Words failed Sebastian once more. They always did when he arrived at the subject of his father's death in distant waters during the Battle of Trafalgar nearly six years past. Though Mama's official mourning period had ended and she had resumed regular dress and social engagements, she still adamantly refused the idea of loving another.

"Naturally, she insisted we come to Jenwick Park at once. I suspect she is sharing the news with Mrs. Dailey now," he added.

Lydia nodded and looked down at the ground. She had been Sebastian's chief source of comfort during his greatest challenge. By now, they knew well that some things were best left to silence.

"He may be blessed with a daughter instead. In that case, you will still be Lord Benning one day."

"Indeed." Sebastian nodded listlessly. "Then again, perhaps this will secure me another decade before Mama truly begins making demands," he added with a rueful chuckle.

"You mustn't wait a decade, Sebastian." Lydia groaned. "Even if you do not inherit the title. Besides, it is not as if you are wanting for opportunity. Ladies throw themselves at you in most disgraceful fashions every Season because of your charming nature—so I have heard. That, I have been unable to verify for myself as yet." She paused, offering a small smile to soften her jest. "Still, it appears you could have your choice even of the young misses coming out this Season."

To Sebastian's surprise, Lydia bumped his arm with her shoulder, a rare display of that lovely freedom he always longed to see more of. If anyone deserved a loosening of the strings, it was Lydia. She possessed a lightning-quick wit that made her particularly adept at teasing, a fact Sebastian admired and often contested. He usually lost, yet the fun of the competition could not be denied.

"Ow, Ellen!" Mercy yelped, one hand clutching her pelisse and the other cradling the back of her bonnet.

"Forgive me, Mercy! I was lost in thought—"

"There, there now, darling," Mercy cooed, still wincing as she took Ellen's hands in hers. "Remember to be watchful of your surroundings. Are you hurt?"

The others flocked to Ellen, surrounding her with words of comfort. Had it been anyone else to knock heads with Mercy, they would have received a proper, though short-lived, scolding.

Sebastian used the distraction to concoct a meager rebuttal. "Truly, Lydia, I have as much time as any man could desire to settle those affairs. My grandfather lived to one hundred years of age. Perhaps I shall do the same," he suggested, evading Lydia's other points.

A lady's potential interest was of no concern to him when he knew himself to act purely out of Society's standard of politeness. If they still took it upon themselves to develop affections or saw something to desire in his family connection, the responsibility lay entirely with them. No lady's particular regard had managed to sway Sebastian's heart yet.

Lydia shook her head again. This time, when she looked up at Sebastian, she wore that even rarer smile that lit her from within. It was not a blinding, overwhelming light. Instead, it was steady and relaxed. Natural.

"Do not think you will get away with outliving me, Sebastian Harrowsmith," she announced, struggling to suppress a laugh. "Who else will suffer to keep you in line?"

Before he could fight it, the thought ran wild. A lifetime of Lydia by his side badgering him about one thing or another. But it would not feel like badgering, not to him. Not when he knew how much love and care stood behind it. Would such a life be so terrible? Surely, Lydia would think so—especially considering her mother's particular interest in marrying her into a direct line of a titled family. No sons of second sons permitted.

Sebastian shook his head, forcing that nonsense out. It had no right being in his mind to begin with, not when he had always known his inheritance came with no guarantee. Yet it was not the loss of the title that had rattled Sebastian so deeply, but that was not for Lydia to know.

"Are you well, Seb—"

"Yes, yes, and who will keep your favorite painter housed and fed so that he may continue to bless us with his gifts?" Sebastian laughed, the sound slicing through the growing discomfort in his stomach. "Tell me, will you finally try to meet Mr. Abel Euston this Season?"

Lydia's free hand flew to her cheek, her eyes round with shock. "Certainly not! Heavens, if I tried to converse with him on his splendid mastery of oils, I would look an utter fool. My own skill is so lacking in comparison, and I do not know nearly enough to be worthy of speaking with an artist of Mr. Euston's caliber."

Sebastian let out a soft laugh, the tension dissolving. This, he could do. "Tell me, then, all of these things you do not know," he prodded. He knew she knew far more than she realized.

"I suppose the first thing one must consider is the brushstroke," Lydia began.

In moments, she had found an easy rhythm, punctuated by questions she often answered for herself. This, Sebastian could do. He could listen to Lydia's words just as much as he could listen to her silences. Forever.

# CHAPTER THREE

LYDIA LONGED FOR nothing more than to relieve her upper back in a deep stretch. Spending the last few days being jostled in a carriage and sleeping in unfamiliar beds did her already stiff muscles no favors. Instead, she held her shoulders uncomfortably straight as she worked at her breakfast of toast with marmalade, silverware whispering against fine china. The first London morning was always the worst.

"The post, madam," a footman announced at the door to the breakfast room. Without disrupting her long and graceful sip of tea, Mother waved the servant in, the ruffled sleeve of her azure morning dress flitting artfully. He delivered tidy stacks of mail to each member of the Dailey family, Lydia included, before seeing himself out in silence.

Though she would much rather continue enjoying this crisp toast, Lydia knew her duty. Just as Father and Edmund folded and stowed their newspapers, Mother and Lydia both set down their cutlery with the utmost care. Several years ago, Mother had granted both Lydia and Edmund the privilege of receiving their letters directly rather than having them inspected and distributed by her. She still insisted they all read their mail together at the table as a proper family should. The sound of rustling parchment filled the breakfast room, each flipping through their portion of the day's letters.

One from Isabel. Another from the Gardiner sisters. Individual ones from Mercy and Felicity. And another from Felicity, likely correcting some mistake or expounding upon a random thought from the first one. Even two of Lydia's London acquaintances had written, no doubt announcing their returns for the Season and their polite wishes to promenade together in the near future.

Lydia's brows twitched as she ran a thumb over the last letter. She did not recognize the handwriting or the name on the outer sheet envelope. The seal, a swan floating within amethyst wax, proved equally ineffectual at providing any information. It was smaller than the rest, folded with crisp, clean lines, yet somehow, it weighed against Lydia's hand, laden with mystery.

"Are you quite well, Lydia?" Father's measured voice cut clear across the room. Lydia kept her jolt of surprise internal, fixing her father with a steady gaze.

"Certainly, Father. I am merely pleased to see that so many of my friends and acquaintances have arrived safely in London."

Mother's eyes darted up from her letter, a terribly long one with writing crammed into the very edges of the paper, most likely from her older, unmarried cousin who was fond of "dreadfully distasteful gossip," as Mother put it. Yet she always read every word; it was only right and respectful of the time and effort given by the writer. Except for when she was too busy focusing her attention on Lydia.

"That is rather an extraordinary number of letters for our first day."

Lydia's heart lurched in her chest. For reasons she did not have time to understand, she wanted nothing more than to keep the odd, little letter to herself.

"Indeed, it does seem that way. But these are all from the Bainbridge neighbors—one each from the Misses Reeve—and a few from ladies I met in London during past Seasons."

"Very good, dearest. How well-liked you are." Father nodded his approval and satisfaction before returning to his newspaper.

Mother pursed her lips and shook her head. She hardly considered her husband's opinion on matters concerning the upbringing of their daughter. "Those Reeve girls. Do they not know one letter for one household will suffice?"

Clearing her throat, Lydia quickly swallowed down a spurt of tepid tea to mask her laugh. "Fe—*Miss Felicity Reeve* simply has much to say," she explained, hurrying over her near mistake. Mother did not like for Lydia or Edmund to call anyone by their Christian names unless they were family. Not even lifelong friends who might as well have been sisters were afforded the privilege.

With one last disapproving murmur, Mother returned to her own mail. Lydia looked down at the still unopened letters in her lap, knots twisting in her stomach. She had already lied. What was breaking one small rule on top of that?

Guilt gnawed at Lydia's insides with ferocious determination as she pretended to read Ellen's and Clara's letters in one hand while slipping the mysterious letter under her napkin with the other. A covert glance up and down the table revealed her parents and brother to be none the wiser.

The rest of breakfast passed at a maddeningly sedate pace, Lydia forcing herself to chew her food thoroughly to prevent choking. Nothing would have been more mortifying than collapsing at the table and allowing Mother to snoop on her private correspondence. As soon as Mother dismissed her from the table, letter deftly hidden amongst the generous folds of her powder-blue morning gown, Lydia raced up the staircase and to her rooms as quickly as her ladylike strides could carry her.

"Good morning, Miss Dailey. Shall I dress you for your first appoint—"

"Not just yet, Mullens." Lydia hurried, thinking quickly and throwing open the trunk at the foot of her bed. "I am afraid this shawl must have snagged on something on the long journey. Would you please see if it can be mended?"

Accepting the lump of fabric, the maid curtseyed and left her mistress to the relief of solitude. Lydia had already broken the seal by the time she settled in at her writing desk. She had to work quickly, not knowing when her maid would return or when another would be sent with some command or question from Mother.

*"Dearest Miss Dailey, if you are reading these words, that means you chose to trust me instead of simply discarding a letter from an unknown source. For that, I thank you."*

Lydia paused. She reread those first sentences again and then held the single sheet of paper out at arm's length, as if someone might jump out from behind it and confess to spying on her this whole time, even reading her thoughts during breakfast. Her skin prickled with an unfamiliar mixture of emotions, from curiosity to dread and everything in between.

*"If you are reading still, that means you have a heart for adventure."*

At this, Lydia allowed herself a modest roll of the eyes. Whoever this was, they clearly did not know her after all.

*"You possess a heart that seeks one thing above all else: true love. And if you accept this admittedly baffling adventure, you may just find yourself in the right place at the right time. Lady Spurgold's welcome ball could very well be the perfect place and time...as long as you know what to look for.*

*"Now, you did not think I would give you all the answers, did you? If your most earnest wish is for love, you must be willing to listen to your heart and trust yourself. However, I will tell you just this. What you do with it is entirely up to you...but something tells me the determined and ever purposeful Miss Dailey is up to the task.*

*"Consider this carefully: Perhaps the one you seek is nearer than you think."*

Every muscle in Lydia froze. It couldn't be.... No, that would be far too obvious. Besides, this could very well be a cruel prank. And if it was not....

That meant someone out there thought her utterly incapable of finding a match on her own and for some unfathomable reason had taken it upon themselves to accomplish the task for her. Lydia let out the breath she'd been holding, allowing herself to slump a little in her chair. The letter hung limply from her fingertips. If that was the case, the anonymous author was not incorrect. Lydia's last four Seasons were proof of that.

Steadying herself, Lydia returned her attention to the last few lines of the letter. Mother always said self-pity was a disgraceful, useless trait. Besides, Lydia knew if she started down that slippery slope, she might just burrow herself under the plush blankets on her bed and spend the rest of the Season hiding away from the world and her fading dreams.

*"Above all, remember that you are exactly who you are meant to be, and your perfect gentleman loves all that you are and everything you have yet to become. If you believe nothing else in this letter, believe this: You are ready."*

An excessively flourishing signature at the bottom of the letter revealed a "Lady Swan" as the writer, a return address nowhere to be found. Lydia narrowed her eyes at the swooping curves and elegant loops, as if willing them into a different configuration she would recognize.

A soft knock at the door jolted her back to reality. She took a moment to reacquaint herself with her familiar London bedroom and its soft, cream wallpaper with delicate pink and purple floral details, the large, four-poster bed in the center, the beautiful seascape painting by Mr. Euston on the opposite wall.

It all looked exactly the same. Yet suddenly, she did not feel the same.

"Miss Dailey? Are you ready for me?" Mullens called from the other side of the door.

"Enter," Lydia called as she pulled open her desk drawer, quickly slipping the letter under the assortment of other letters she had saved from her friends over the years.

"Fixed that shawl right up for you, miss." The maid slipped into the room, brandishing the lilac muslin fabric across her arms like an offering.

Lydia accepted it and pretended to inspect Mullens's handiwork as the maid laid out several options for walking dresses, all in various shades of blue. Really, it had only been the beginnings of a frayed edge and she had much else to occupy her mind than one shawl out of the dozens in her collection.

"Thank you, Mullens. Marvelous work, as always." Lydia eyed the dress in the middle. "The light blue with the pleats on the bodice and the ruffles at the hem." She always wore the same color throughout the day, no matter how many times she changed.

As the maid worked to make her mistress presentable for her first few appointments of the day, Lydia rattled her mind for any possible connections to a Lady Swan. No matter how long or hard she thought, nothing sparked. She even considered the other young ladies she'd met over the years who now bore their husbands' names and titles. Still, no one claimed the name of Lady Swan in her memory.

"There," Mullens announced with triumph as she pinned the last brown curl in place. "You are ready."

Lydia focused once more. Her own icy-blue eyes stared back at her through the mirror of her vanity. This strange disconnect of being lost in thought did not suit her. It took a moment more for Mullens's words to sink in.

"What did you say?" Lydia demanded, twisting around in the low-backed chair.

The maid shuffled back a few steps in surprise. "I-I only said that you are ready for the day, miss."

"Of course." Lydia nodded, turned back to the mirror, and composed herself. No servant would risk their livelihood to interfere so boldly in the affairs of the family they served—especially not the Dailey family. "That is all thanks to you, dear Mullens." She smiled at the young woman, somewhere around Lydia's age, through the glass. Mullens smiled back, a proud blush coloring her pale cheeks.

*"You are ready."*

Those words echoed in Lydia's mind. If what this letter proposed was real and there was someone out there guiding Lydia to love…was she truly ready?

# CHAPTER FOUR

CHANDELIERS GLITTERED AND dresses glimmered everywhere the eye landed in Lady Spurgold's ballroom. Lydia glanced down at her own ivory gown threaded with silver embroidery, an unusual nest of anxious butterflies astir in her stomach.

If her mysterious benefactor, Lady Swan, was correct, tonight could very well change Lydia's life. Tonight could be the night she met her husband.

*"Perhaps the one you seek is nearer than you think."*

That one line continued to tug at the back of Lydia's mind, drowning out the music others danced to. Silken fingers twisting around each other, she pressed her back against a dazzling floral arrangement bursting with blush pinks and lively corals that no doubt outshone Lydia and spoke highly of the countess's extravagant taste.

The simplest interpretation of Lady Swan's words pointed to a gentleman she already knew. Yet considering the entire male population of her world consisted of her father, her brother, and her brother's boisterous bachelor friends, Lydia had no options for suitors.

And then there was Sebastian.

Lydia shook her head, more of a twitch, in truth. She could not risk dislodging the diamonds, pearls, and plumes of feathers meticulously nestled in her intricate coiffure. A passing old gentleman eyed her quizzically and moved on, more or less reassured by Lydia's offered smile. At least Mother stood several feet away, distracted by a highly desirable conversation including Lady Spurgold herself. Lydia could not bear her reprimands and criticisms as well as the inane ideas planted in her head by that blasted letter.

Besides, there was nothing about Sebastian. They had grown up together, old childhood friends—a deep, strong bond, set in its ways.

Composing herself, Lydia looked out toward the dance floor in the center of the ballroom, crowded with prancing couples who could be falling in love at that very moment. She supposed Lady Swan might be alluding to one of her almost-suitors of the past, a gentleman with whom she'd shared a dance or walk or carriage ride who had ultimately abandoned her dour complexion in favor of greener pastures with bright eyes and smiles to spare.

Had one of them experienced a change of heart? Had Lydia been weighing on someone's mind? The mere possibility that she might have unknowingly captured someone's affections sent a shiver of foolish anticipation down her spine.

"Lydia, there you are! Thank goodness, I had nearly gone mad."

Sebastian's voice just behind her sent the shiver back the way it had come, all the way up to Lydia's head. It ricocheted, making her dizzy as she turned around to face her oldest friend.

He grinned, candlelight casting a halo around his dark hair. "Please tell me you have not already promised yourself for the next set."

"I have not, Mr. Harrowsmith," Lydia replied, careful to use proper address where anyone might hear. She lifted her chin into the air. "If you wish to change that, you had best ask properly."

"Very well." Sebastian groaned. Even his exasperation sounded good-natured. He grasped Lydia's gloved hand and bent low over it, his eyes remaining on her face. "Will you do me the honor of sharing this dance with me, Miss Dailey?"

Lydia stared back for a long moment. "Perhaps." She sighed,

elegantly tossing her head.

"That is not fair," Sebastian argued, standing up and tugging at the lapels of his handsome, dark-blue coat. "If I must ask properly, then you must answer properly."

"Is it not the lady's prerogative to choose her answer?" Lydia fought a smile, daring Sebastian to challenge her from the corner of her eye.

Sebastian frowned and lifted a shoulder in a shrug. "Then I suppose you have had your fill of dancing for the night? If you decline me, you must decline all other men. Surely, you do not wish to begin the Season on the wall?"

Lydia's smile slipped away. She had forgotten how enjoyable it was to not be thinking about Lady Swan's letter. Of course Sebastian was right. She was in no position to be denying anyone if she had any hope of following the would-be matchmaker's clues to her happy ending.

"Lyd—"

The music crescendoed and ceased. A polite round of applause echoed through Lord and Lady Spurgold's ballroom. The couples, divided into neat rows, bowed and curtseyed to each other before hurrying off to the edges of the room for refreshments.

"Has your 'perhaps' become a 'yes,' Miss Dailey?"

"You are too silly, Mr. Harrowsmith," Lydia mumbled.

Sebastian held out his hand, palm up. A knowing expectation glinted in his eyes. Lydia accepted, his long fingers engulfing hers, and allowed Sebastian to lead her onto the dance floor.

The music began, soft and lilting at first as the pairs circled each other. Lydia could already see Sebastian trying to read her. How he always managed to sense the acutest changes in her mood, she could not guess.

"Does something trouble you, Lydia?" he asked the moment his left hand caught hers, his right hand landing on her waist.

Indecision seized her for only a moment. As pitiful as the confession of receiving such a letter might have been, it was one sure way to cross a potentiality from Lydia's meager list.

"If I tell you, you must promise not to laugh," she mumbled under her breath, glancing around to be sure the nearby couples were all enraptured with each other and the dance.

Sebastian's face grew uncharacteristically serious. Lydia could even feel his grip tighten on her ever so slightly, urging her closer. "I would never dare make light of anything that troubles you."

Heat prickled under the curls at the nape of Lydia's neck. She offered a prayer of thanks as the dance momentarily pulled them apart and paired them with different partners. She could not have borne the intensity in his gaze for a moment longer, not with all this other nonsense weighing on her. That would only invite confusion and mixed signals. No, it was best Lydia rule out Sebastian here and now, once and for all.

Lydia's temporary partner gave her a twirl that elegantly carried her across the room back to Sebastian. He took her in his arms once more, familiar despite the tingling across the surface of her skin.

"I have had a letter," she announced quietly, tilting her face up. Sebastian anticipated her movement and lowered his head down, aligning her lips with his ear.

A black lock tickled the tip of Lydia's nose. She quickly pulled back, realizing her mistake. She need not get *quite* so close to convey information. Instead, she fixed her gaze on the spot between his thick brows so she need not look him directly in the eye. Somehow, that seemed just as unbearable, as intimate.

"You as well? It has been a strange time for communications. What kind of letter did you receive?" Sebastian prompted, frowning in a thoughtful, mildly concerned way. Lydia forced her eyes to the gleaming, wooden floor and the tips of her slippers peeking out from the hem of her evening gown.

She took in a deep breath and exhaled it in a sigh. "I will remind you that you promised not to laugh," she started.

It took the better part of the dance for Lydia to explain the contents of the letter. The steps, graceful though they were, forced them apart and down the line or into other formations a frustrating number of times.

"Well, what do you make of it?" Lydia finally managed to ask. "Could it be…a gentleman from last Season?" The nerves coiled in her stomach had worked themselves into quite a storm after having to explain Lady Swan's letter piecemeal over the course of the dance, redirecting the aim of her question. Lydia had never considered herself to be particularly brave. She certainly was not brave enough to ask what she truly wanted to know. Not yet.

The stabilizing pressure of Sebastian's hands on her disappeared as he released her and took a step back. It took Lydia a beat too long to realize that the music had stopped. The dance had ended.

She shuffled back to her place in the line of ladies and curtseyed in one fluid movement with the others to the bowing gentlemen lined up on the other side of the dance floor. Sebastian never removed his eyes from her as he marched straight toward Lydia while the other dancers either lingered for another set or scurried away for a rest.

"Mr. Harrowsmith!"

He stopped mid-step, his head turning at the same time as Lydia's to find a young lady approaching from the opposite side of the room. She was so petite, she had to crane her neck back to get a proper view of Sebastian's face, lovely light-brown curls bouncing.

The ambient conversation buzzing throughout the room prevented Lydia from hearing the remainder of that particular one, yet she could tell well enough when a young lady believed she had been spurned. Sebastian nodded his head in farewell and continued toward Lydia. The woman turned away, clasped hands falling to her sides and head lowering. For just a breath, Lydia marveled at her ability to reveal any emotion in such a crowded room.

"Another?" Sebastian asked the moment he was within earshot, just nearly dodging a blissfully oblivious couple jaunting onto the dance floor.

"Who is that charming young lady?" Lydia prodded, flashing her eyes toward the pretty woman in the spring-green gown staring wistfully into a glass of punch.

Shaking his head, Sebastian held a hand out to Lydia. "Just Miss Woods. We met late last Season. I promised I would try to converse with her later."

Lydia arched a brow. "I do not think Miss Woods merely wished to converse. She was hoping for a dance."

Sebastian shrugged. "We are at Lord and Lady Spurgold's welcome ball. There will never be a stronger concentration of eligible gentlemen in one room for Miss Woods to dance with for the rest of the Season."

Despite her frown, Lydia accepted her friend's hand and followed him back to the center of the resplendent ballroom. "I am not sure if you are being intentionally or unintentionally obtuse, nor am I sure which is worse."

"Does it matter?" Sebastian laughed. "The end result is the same. Miss Woods will have to find other means of entertaining herself tonight. I have grander designs for my evening."

As if for his own personal dramatic effect, the musicians plunged into a sprightly tune. Sebastian tilted his head to one side, a triumphant smile stretched across his face as he sank back into the line of gentlemen—though Lydia could hardly fathom what had him so smug.

"And what designs are those?" she asked when they came together.

Sebastian scoffed. "Why, helping you solve Lady Swan's riddle, of course."

Of course. *Of course.* Those two simple words chased themselves through Lydia's mind. Well, Sebastian had answered her original query.

There could be no way Lady Swan intended for her message to guide Lydia toward Sebastian. Not if he seemed so enthused about helping her decipher it.

If he had been the answer, there would be no riddle to solve.

"Do you have any theories yet?"

Lydia's mind snapped back into focus. She stared back at her friend's inquisitive smile and shook her head. "No. None."

"A shame," he said with an exaggerated groan that did not hide a strange flash across his eyes. "If we had unraveled it tonight, you could have spent the remainder of the Season laughing at me from your happily wedded throne."

Sebastian spent the remainder of the dance questioning Lydia about the gentlemen she'd met in past Seasons and trying to align her lackluster answers with bits and pieces of Lady Swan's letter. By the dance's end, Lydia had managed to thwart her friend's every suggestion, though he insisted on keeping all her choices open this early in "the hunt," as he himself had called it.

"Really, Lydia, we have only been at it for a mere half hour. We simply need more time. Something is bound to dawn on one of us," Sebastian said, though his smile did not quite reach his eyes, as he led Lydia toward a partially obscured sideboard laden with the finest sweets, fruits, cheeses, and meats.

"Now here is a perspective I had not considered," Sebastian started the moment he untangled his arm from hers.

Lydia glowered internally as he rattled on about perspectives she suddenly cared little to contemplate. She knew she should have been thankful for Sebastian's willingness to throw his whole being into helping her find happiness. For some reason, though, it had soured her outlook on the letter, her interest waning.

She finally interrupted her friend's ramblings with an exasperated sigh. "For heaven's sake, please just fetch me a plate of grapes and strawberries and cheese."

Sebastian's mouth fell open. "Anything for you, dearest Lydia. Poor thing. You must be famished." Without another word, the gentleman rushed to the very end of the table and began piling fresh fruits atop a polished silver plate.

"Miss Lydia…."

The vaguely familiar voice at her back nearly caused Lydia to jump in fright. Instead she mastered her reaction into a delicate turn of the head, eyes wide with mild surprise.

"Lydia Dailey," she answered the lady, the same one who had been trying to secure Sebastian's name on her dance card.

A nasty flip in Lydia's stomach caused a flood of heat to race up her spine and into her cheeks. This complete stranger had heard a young man use her given name *with* a term of endearment! And she had taken such care to choose a less crowded corner of the room to avoid onlookers and eavesdropping.

Yet Lydia would never show that utter embarrassment on her face, even if it resembled ripe tomato more than blushing miss. Keeping her eyes steadily fixed on the other woman, she opened her own blank dance card and fanned herself. Surely, no one would find it odd that she'd become flushed after dancing two sets back to back. This lady need not think otherwise.

"May I help you, Miss...?"

"Emily Woods," the woman replied, glancing furtively to Sebastian, who had made it halfway down the table and had already rather overwhelmed the small plate.

"A pleasure to make your acquaintance." Lydia gave a shallow curtsey, even if the introduction had not occurred through the proper channels.

"My timing leaves much to be desired." Miss Woods chuckled, fidgeting with the end of the white, satin sash around her waist—a habit Mother would have berated out of her long ago. "I have been trying to capture Mr. Harrowsmith just for a moment, just a word. He is a rather swift gentleman, is he not?"

Lydia turned away from the evident longing in Miss Woods's eyes, watching the gently swirling liquid rippling against her glass. "Indeed he is. Too swift, some might say."

At that, Miss Woods's attention returned back to Lydia. Red-tinged brown ringlets perfectly framed the young lady's round face. "H-How are you acquainted with Mr. Harrowsmith, if I may ask?"

"I am merely an old friend. We grew up on adjoining properties in Bainbridge in Kent. Our families have known each other for a very long time," Lydia answered with a polite smile.

Miss Woods contemplated that information, eyeing Lydia up and down. She returned a smile of relief, perhaps having weighed her physical attributes against Lydia's and coming to the conclusion that hers would tip the scales in her favor. Or perhaps she had heard of unmarried Miss Lydia Dailey and realized that if a close friend like Sebastian had not proposed to her by her fourth Season, he likely had no desire to graduate from friendship.

"Here you are. Ah, Miss Woods, so good of you to join us." Sebastian wore an accommodating smile as he approached the pair of ladies, clutching Lydia's nearly overflowing plate in both hands.

"Mr. Harrowsmith," Miss Woods cooed. "I hoped to have a word."

Sebastian nodded understandingly. "I must apologize that our timing seems to be amiss tonight, Miss Woods, but I am afraid I will have to ask your leave to save that word for another time? Miss Dailey and I are embroiled in a fascinating mystery. Nothing to be alarmed by, surely." His rejection was perfectly polite, if a little overly thorough.

Lydia had to admire the girl. She flipped her crushing disappointment into bashful hope in an instant, far quicker than Sebastian would notice, certainly.

"Of course, another time, then. I look forward to it." Miss Woods curtseyed gracefully and excused herself, slipping into the crowd.

"Goodness, I hardly remember where we left off. Do you?" Sebastian took a long sip from the glass he'd just plucked from a passing footman's tray. "No matter. You should eat first, Lydia." He gestured toward her untouched plate with his drink.

Glancing at Miss Woods's retreating form, Lydia grumbled, "Sebastian." She suppressed the urge to snap her fan in the palm of her hand as her mother did when she or Edmund failed to comprehend or act on her orders quickly enough.

"Yes?" His warm, brown eyes darted up to meet her gaze, one hand still outstretched toward the mound of plump grapes.

Now Lydia fought the laugh bubbling up from some deep and warm place in her chest. Goodness, how could Sebastian still look so much like the little boy for whom she had kept watch while he'd snuck into the kitchens of the much more relaxed Creeves Abbey? They would have never dared to do such a thing in the Dailey home, of course.

"I promise I only meant to steal just one. And I had nearly managed it, too."

"Not that," she sputtered, smacking his hand away and plucking a grape for herself. "*Her.*" Lydia subtly pointed with her chin in the direction Miss Woods had gone.

Sebastian wrinkled his nose and stood to his full height. "What of Miss Woods?"

"You should speak with her."

The gentleman took a deep, slow inhale, his broad chest filling out his handsomely embroidered vest and coat. "I have spoken with her before and that conversation did not inspire me to seek out another."

Lydia's brows plunged into a severe furrow. Slipping the grape into her mouth, she chewed furiously and swallowed with purpose. "After a single conversation? She might surprise you, you know. At least give Miss Woods that chance."

Instead of heeding her excellent advice, her friend took a step closer, bringing them almost toe to toe. He smiled down at her. "I know without a doubt that I will not find a better conversation than the one we are having right now."

Foolish though it was, the declaration left Lydia speechless, even when he stole a cube of cheese with a mischievous half-smile.

Why should she have been flattered? Sebastian was no stranger to such turns of phrase. They were friends, after all, and he came from a family fond of expressing any emotion from the mundane to the borderline theatrical. He said such flowery things with regularity.

"I suppose I must oblige you since you are such a champion for Miss Woods," Sebastian continued. "My mother will certainly appreciate your efforts. I trust your plate will be far emptier when I return." With a smile and nod, Sebastian left Lydia with the treats for which she no longer had an appetite.

The longer she watched Sebastian weave through the maze of guests, the less it made sense for the letter writer to choose such an obvious target as Sebastian.

There was no suspense or art in it. Only an unexplainable, dull ache in her chest when she watched Sebastian return to the dance floor with Miss Woods on his arm.

As the dance began, the lady positively beaming now that she had finally secured her long-awaited moment with her chosen gentleman, Lydia began to regret Lady Swan's letter most of all for the strange notion it had put in her head regarding Sebastian.

Odd that a plainly incorrect interpretation would rattle Lydia so when she had never once spared a moment to consider Sebastian in such a light. The mere idea that his carefree heart would fall in love with her austere disposition had always seemed the height of absurdity.

"Lydia, at last!"

A welcome voice dragged Lydia from her sullen reverie. The world shimmered again as Isabel rounded the impressive floral arrangement to Lydia's right, Ellen and Clara following, their families already dispersing throughout the ballroom. All three looked stunning in gowns of blush and matching muted yellow for the sisters. Lydia happily turned her attention away from all thoughts of Lady Swan and Sebastian as her friends surrounded her.

"You know how dear Maria is always charging ahead without looking. Well, now she has had a shocking tumble down the stairs, earlier this evening while we were all readying ourselves for the ball," Isabel explained in a rush. "She was assessed by a physician right away and is perfectly well besides a twisted ankle.

Aunt Matilda generously elected to remain home with Maria tonight so the rest of us could come; the little darling is still shaken by it all."

Lydia removed the hand she had pressed to her heart and took Isabel's. "It is such a relief to hear that your sweet sister will make a full recovery. And what of you two?" She turned to the Gardiner girls. It was not like their family to be this fashionably late to such an illustrious event.

Ellen and Clara exchanged uneasy glances. "Nicholas only drove us as far as the Abbotts' home, leaving us to take advantage of their familiarity and kindness in transporting us the rest of the way. Poor Mama was mortified."

Pursing her lips, Lydia nodded as if such rude behavior made any sense. She supposed it did when she considered Ellen's and Clara's older brother and his fondness for finding himself on the losing end of bets. Apparently, spending nearly a decade as the current head of the Gardiner household, and a few before that assisting with its management as their father's health had declined, still had not inspired the necessary sense of responsibility in young Mr. Nicholas Gardiner.

At least that was what Lydia had heard whispered around their Bainbridge neighbors and mutual London acquaintances. The man had likely abandoned his mother and sisters to beg for transportation from friends so he could arrive at some gambling hall or other in comfort and style.

"Have you had any dances yet?" Isabel asked, slipping a fan from her reticule and swiftly waving it before her face, wisps of black hair fluttering.

"Just two with Sebastian."

"And Mercy and Felicity? Where are they?"

Lydia nodded toward the center of the room, two bright-blonde heads on opposite ends bobbing up and down gracefully. "Lady Eldmar has kept them on their feet all night."

Unfortunately for Lydia, the steps of the dance necessitated that Sebastian and his partner quickly cross the floor, spinning in a beautiful pattern past Lydia's line of sight. Her gaze followed, a small frown forcing its way onto her lips.

"Lydia dear, are you unwell?" Ellen whispered. As usual, she appeared just beside Lydia in complete silence, like a shadow come to life.

There was nothing for it. Lydia took a deep inhale and glanced at the small circle of friends surrounding her. "Despite my dislike of mystery and surprises, one seems to have landed in my lap. Will you all help me solve it, if it can indeed be solved?"

Each girl's eyes sparked at the idea. Clara's mouth fell open in a delighted smile. Lydia could see all the questions she did not want to answer in the middle of a crowded ballroom on the tip of the younger Gardiner sister's tongue. Her hand shot up, silencing Clara just in time. Instead, she bit down on her bottom lip, not the most elegant or proper solution for the setting, but far better than the alternative.

"We likely will not have an opportunity to discuss it tonight, I am afraid," Lydia said, lowering her voice and dipping her head down. Her friends followed suit, creating their own little conspiratorial bubble. "It must wait until our luncheon. There is no moving forward without Felicity and Mercy, after all."

"But that is in two days!" Clara hissed, the agony of impatience crumpling her doll-like face. "You mean to keep us in suspense for two days?"

Lydia huffed. "It is not two full days. Besides, this is not the most conducive environment for a complex conversation."

She subtly gestured to her right at a nearby group of older gentlemen laughing and slapping each other on the shoulder, drinks sloshing dangerously in their glasses. No matter where they went in this lavishly spacious room, they would find no true privacy or peace. They would have to quit the ballroom entirely, and that they could not do without a chaperone. The only one likely to have allowed them some alone time in an empty sitting room with the door ajar was Lady Ainsworth, Isabel's Aunt Matilda.

"At luncheon, then," Isabel agreed, shooting Clara a stern look.

The youngest of their group groaned and wrinkled her nose before sighing in resignation. "Very well. At luncheon."

In one fluid movement, all four ladies lifted their heads at the same time and returned their attention to their surroundings. Once again, Lydia had the misfortune of immediately noticing Sebastian and Miss Woods on the dance floor. She certainly noticed the way he nodded along at his partner's every word, smiling all the while. Sebastian's smile widened as he laughed at some clever remark or amusing anecdote. Lydia shook her head.

How could she already need reminding that Sebastian himself had removed any possibility that he was her intended? How could she have even entertained the thought that Sebastian might be happy with a stern disposition like hers when he was clearly capable of having an enjoyable evening full of conversation and laughter without her?

"Are you sure you are quite well, darling?" Isabel asked, puncturing Lydia's rogue thoughts.

She cleared her throat and this time chose a lie. "Of course."

# CHAPTER FIVE

SEBASTIAN GROANED AND raised his arms high into the air, coattails riding up. He always found himself stiff and in need of frequent stretches the morning after a ball. Taking up his newspaper once more, he settled into the peace of his favorite wing-backed chair after a boisterous breakfast with his younger brothers.

"Good morning, dear," Mama chirped in the doorway, still wearing her burgundy robe and cap after taking her breakfast in bed.

"Good morning, Mama," he offered in response, leaving behind his newspaper once more to cross the room and escort his mother to her usual spot on the sofa.

"Where are my other lovely sons?" she asked as she settled into her embroidery and Sebastian resumed his seat.

"Peter is off to his club and then Astley's and Anthony has returned to bed, I believe." He chuckled, easing back into his chair. His mother always brought a calm, grounding presence to the room.

"Tell me, how was Lady Spurgold's ball, Sebastian? I did not manage to catch you last night when you returned home, but Peter told me that you danced twice with Miss Dailey—unsurprising, I suppose—and also seemed to be having quite a lively time with a Miss Woods?"

Sebastian hid his grimace behind his newspaper. He had been

hoping to avoid mention of Lydia for as long as possible. Sleep had evaded him for what had felt like an eternity despite the late hour. Balls always tended to burn the candle down to a nub. The lack of rest had certainly not helped his stiffness this morning.

The rest of Mama's statement faded into the background. Sebastian's mind had been drawn right back to Lydia's anonymous benefactor. What a truly bizarre situation, indeed! One that did not bode well for him. He answered the rest of Mama's questions to the best of his ability, guilt tugging at him for his lackluster answers. Yet now that he had Lydia and this supposed Lady Swan's letter in his sights again, he would not easily let it go.

*"Perhaps the one you seek is nearer than you think."*

*"Above all, remember that you are exactly who you are meant to be, and your perfect gentleman loves all that you are and everything you have yet to become."*

Eyes unfocusing, the sharp, black letters printed on the pages before him blurred into the bits and pieces Lydia had shared with him from memory last night. Sebastian's jaw clenched as he sank deeper into thought. It seemed impossible to tell if the letter's contents were genuine or how they could begin to trace it to its origins. At least the writer's intentions appeared to be good for now, though Sebastian personally found her methods to be unique at best and disturbing at worst. Lady Swan wrote as if she knew Lydia, knew what was best for her.

Sebastian's fingers gripped his newspaper tighter. As Lydia had recited the letter in bits and pieces during their dance, a faint glimmer of hope had begun to pulse in that deep part of Sebastian's heart that he kept locked away. Who could Lady Swan mean if not him?

According to Lydia, almost anyone else. It had quickly become evident that the thought of Lady Swan leading her to her best friend had not seemed to enter Lydia's mind. When Sebastian thought back on it now, he could hardly fathom why he'd so foolishly allowed himself to think he could take that place.

It had taken every ounce of strength Sebastian had to zealously leap into the mystery with her as a supportive friend should. He wanted Lydia to have all the happiness and love she deserved, especially after the disappointments of past Seasons. With the anonymous writer offering her sage assistance, Lydia now stood on the precipice of all that she desired. Sebastian would not hinder her chances.

"Sebastian? What article are you reading that has you so engrossed?"

He started and folded the top of the newspaper back to find Mama watching him with a quizzical look, her embroidery needle still pinched between her thumb and forefinger. Swallowing against the sudden dryness in his throat, Sebastian blurted out, "A new shoemaker will be opening a shop not far from here next week."

"A new shoemaker is what's got you so excited?" Mama sighed with a bemused smile. "And here I thought perhaps you had seen the dreadful announcement of an engagement."

Sebastian narrowed his eyes at Mama. "Forgive me, but how would that be better than a new shoemaker?"

The older woman glanced about the morning room and gave an almost imperceptible shrug. "At least it would mean that you had taken an interest in someone. I know you are still young and that many gentlemen choose to delay marriage, but you are in a unique position as it is with your new cousin—"

Sebastian interrupted, offering a strained smile. "You need not remind me, Mama." In the past, he had not minded her good-natured prods, few and far between. Since the arrival of his uncle's letter, Mama's interest in Sebastian's future had grown increasingly urgent. The child could be a girl, after all, as the entire *ton* seemed fond of reminding him when the unfortunate topic came about. At least the baron and his new bride had elected to remain in the country due to her delicate condition, far from potentially awkward interactions and judgements.

"You young men require much reminding about many things." Mama sighed, a fond glow in her eyes.

Sebastian's expression softened. "I am only waiting for the happiness derived from true love, I promise."

"Certainly, my son. I am praying for that every day." Setting aside her embroidery, Mama leaned across the small table between her sofa and Sebastian's chair and grasped his hand for a moment. At least she still managed to restrain herself once he'd made his feelings clear.

Sebastian knew he was young, just three-and-twenty, not a full month younger than Lydia. He also knew that even wealthy and titled men who prolonged bachelorhood did sometimes struggle to compete seriously in the marriage mart. New waves of gentlemen with the handsomeness of youth on their sides flooded in every Season. As a mother with one desirable marriage added to her family's lineage thus far, that of Sebastian's older sister, Mama certainly knew the same.

Surely, if he could only ask Papa... Sebastian cleared his parched throat and flicked his newspaper back up to cover his face and reached for his cup of tea. Such wishful thinking did him no good. He had learned that long ago in the deepest days of his grief after Papa had heroically fallen in battle. Lydia had been by his side the entire time, leaving him be when he needed it, letting him rant against the unfairness of it all...even holding his hand on those days when the tears seemed never-ending.

Miss Lydia Dailey, holding the hand of a gentleman she had no intention of marrying. Such a thought would have been shocking, near unthinkable, for those who knew her. All except Sebastian.

"Mama," he said quietly, folding his newspaper away. "What do you think of Lydia?" The question was out before Sebastian could wonder what had possessed him to ask it.

Chewing on her bottom lip thoughtfully, Mama finished pulling her needle through the white cloth and set aside her colorful bouquet of thread. "What do I think of Miss Dailey? How do you mean?"

"In a general sense," Sebastian said hurriedly with what he

hoped passed as a nonchalant shrug. They had just been talking about marriage and true love, after all. He did not need to instill any other ideas in Mama's head. They would be just as difficult to dislodge from hers as they were from his own.

The woman frowned. "She has indeed been such a wonderful friend to you all these years, but I do sometimes wonder how you tolerate each other so well. Your temperaments are so vastly different."

Sebastian's spine prickled. "Perhaps we bring balance to each other," he mumbled, a sudden need to defend himself springing up against Mama's harmless and objectively correct observation. What other answer had he been expecting?

"Of course you do," Mama agreed, taking Sebastian's hand once more. "And I would be remiss if I did not mention that I would adore a daughter-in-law who is just as respectful, well-mannered, and intelligent as Miss Dailey."

"Mama!" Deflating, Sebastian sank down deep in his chair, draping his newspaper over his face and chest. At least this way he could hide his undeserved disappointment—and a strange surge of pride at Mama's admiration of Lydia—behind childishness.

"There, I am done with my speeches at least for today," she insisted, bringing both hands over her heart, though she could not quite hide her amused smile.

"Thank goodness. Much more of that and I would have run out onto the street and proposed to the first woman my eyes landed upon," Sebastian grumbled. He reached across the table and rested his hand over hers. Mama meant well and only wanted what was best for the family after all the challenges they'd faced. He could hardly fault her for that.

"Heavens, no." Mama laughed, fine lines appearing at the corners of her eyes. "I would rather wait another decade for you to marry a lady who leaves me with no doubt that she is worthy of you."

"Even I do not wish to remain unmarried ten years hence."

Sebastian ignored the latter half of Mama's kind statement. She would argue with him to her last breath if he insisted on the truth: that *he* was the unworthy one.

A wistful knot embedded itself in Sebastian's throat. Perhaps now that Lydia had started on her own adventure, he should, too.

No lady had managed to catch his eye yet, despite their fluttering lashes and tasteful swoons. Sebastian was not ignorant of his position as an eligible bachelor. Even if the Benning title did not pass to him, his family still possessed enough wealth to live very comfortably amongst the *ton*, though not quite as comfortably as the handsomely affluent Daileys. Yet no matter how hard he tried, how pleased he knew Mama would be, Sebastian could not tolerate the thought of marrying any of those ladies for one simple reason.

He knew he would not love them.

As Mama had so rightly pointed out, whether she'd intended to or not, Sebastian would never be the one Lydia needed. His best option was to find someone who could emulate her qualities. Mama still remained ignorant to a particularly crucial fact. Indeed, Sebastian sometimes seemed to be the only one aware of it.

Any woman *like* Lydia could only be second to Lydia.

# Chapter Six

Five pairs of softly clicking shoes down the hall announced the girls' arrival. Finally, after two anxious days and securing Mother's approval for a luncheon, Lydia could share the contents of the letter with her dearest friends and join their minds to uncover its secrets.

They spilled into the conservatory. It was a favorite location of Lydia's in their London townhouse, always alive with something green, spots of colorful flowers calling out and catching the eye. Tucked away at the back of the building and shielded by exotic shrubbery, the conservatory afforded Lydia and her guests the privacy they required for all manner of youthful whispering.

"Out with it at once, Lydia," Felicity demanded as soon as the butler had closed the glass doors behind them. Eyes ablaze, she crossed her arms over her pink bodice.

"It truly was cruel of you to offer something as tantalizing as a mysterious matchmaker called 'Lady Swan' to us just as you quit Lady Spurgold's ball for the night," Mercy added, mirroring her sister's expression. More particular about her manners, the younger twin kept her hands politely laced behind her back.

"Perhaps you should consider asking Lady Eldmar with more force to grant you periods of rest during balls," Lydia reasoned. Ever the gracious hostess, she waved her arm toward the delicious array of fruits, cold meats, and pastries spread across the table. "I couldn't find a more convenient opportunity to share the news with you because none of you ceased dancing."

Lydia's friends situated themselves around the table, perching on the edges of their chairs. Each was a graceful, kind, handsome lady deserving of the happiness she desired. Perhaps if Lady Swan could help Lydia, she could help the other Bainbridge girls.

"I am afraid there is no force strong enough to deter the viscountess now that she has become the personal champion for our marriages this Season," Mercy stated frankly.

"Then allow me to distract you from your aching feet and earn your forgiveness all at once," Lydia announced, allowing a brow to rise in dramatic suspense.

Every eye in the conservatory focused on Lydia. Her friends leaned in close, some abandoning half-full plates. She revealed the letter with a flourish.

"Read it!" Felicity cried.

"No, have Clara read it," Isabel suggested as she popped a strawberry into her mouth.

Lydia nodded. "Yes, I think we would all prefer that." Their vibrant Clara was the best at reading aloud, emotional and moving without devolving into farce.

With a gleeful grin, the girl eagerly rose to the occasion. She dropped her cake onto her plate as she rushed to the head of the table to take Lydia's place. Lydia passed the letter to her friend and took a seat beside Ellen. Clearing her throat, Clara held out the single sheet and began to read it for her audience. The cheeks of all the ladies in the conservatory bloomed pink. Halfway through, Lydia wondered if perhaps she should have kept to her original plan of having her friends read it silently and individually. Hearing Lady Swan's words out loud in another's voice reignited the flame of embarrassment in Lydia's stomach.

"'Yours truly, Lady Swan,'" Clara finished in a jumble, swiftly folding up the letter and placing it next to Lydia's plate before scurrying back to her own seat.

A long moment of silence echoed off the glass walls of the

conservatory and whispered through the leaves shielding them from unwanted eyes. The ladies sipped at their tea, each pondering Lady Swan's words—except for Lydia, who had done more than enough of her own fruitless considering. Instead, she gave into her anxiety just a touch and fidgeted with the ivory napkin heaped in her lap.

"I thought it was wonderfully romantic."

The quiet yet confident declaration from Ellen surprised them all. Lydia turned to her friend, a rush of relief engulfing her. She had been starting to wonder if the letter had offended them. "Truly?"

The reassuring smile and hopeful glint in Ellen's eyes answered Lydia first. "Truly. Whoever wrote this is quite poetic and thoughtful. And most importantly—only in my humble opinion, of course—she is optimistic. She believes in our dear Lydia."

Warmth eased the tension in Lydia's chest as she reached over to grasp her friend's hand. "Thank you, Ellen."

"I take it none of you are masquerading as Lady Swan, then?" Mercy added, looking around the table as she cut up a slice of ham.

Every lady besides Lydia shook their heads. Of course Lydia had very briefly considered that one of the Bainbridge girls might have gotten a fancy idea in her head to play matchmaker. One of their favorite girlhood activities had been covertly pointing out handsome boys and whispering in each other's ears about being swept off their feet in the most fantastical ways.

Lydia had dismissed the possibility of her friends' involvement early on. They all knew better than to give each other false hope in the marriage mart.

"I thought that unlikely as well," said Isabel. "Have you any theories on Lady Swan's identity?"

"Lady Swan?" Felicity scoffed. "Should we not be trying to discover the identity of Lydia's promised husband?" The viscount's daughter draped an arm across her forehead and leaned back in her chair, swooning to theatrical perfection. Sitting up, she added, "At least I have already dismissed Lady Spurgold as a suspect."

It took all of Lydia's willpower to keep her eyes from bulging and her mouth from spewing tepid tea across the table. "Felicity Reeve, for heaven's sake, do not tell me you accused Lady Spurgold at her own ball!"

Nightmarish visions spun through Lydia's head of her friend jabbing a finger in Lady Spurgold's face before all her guests while exclaiming the name of Lydia Dailey. Their family would suffer the cut direct on the streets of London as the *ton* turned their noses up at them, forever excluding them from the good graces they had enjoyed for so long. Mother would throw Lydia onto the steps of Jenwick Place and lock the door behind her.

Felicity barked a laugh and shook her head. "Of course not! Impatient and heedless I may be, but I am no fool. I merely engaged her with compliments on the successful evening, particularly the many happy couples dancing as gracefully as swans. She gave no indication that that word carried any significance for her."

Lydia exhaled and leaned back in her chair for just a moment to recover from the surge of horror that had seized her. "Well done, my friend. Well done, indeed."

"Please, may we return to the gentleman question?" Clara set her teacup down, eyes wide. "Is it not obvious? Of course Lady Swan must mean none other than Mr. Harrowsmith."

"Brilliant, Clara!" Felicity cheered. Wearing a grin, she rose from her chair so quickly, it nearly toppled back onto the polished floor as she planted her palms firmly on the table. "I am envious I did not suggest it first. You and Mr. Harrowsmith have always been particular friends. Whoever this Lady Swan is has sorely underestimated us."

Felicity beamed with pride as if she had singlehandedly solved the riddle. The others nodded quickly, turning to Lydia in unison.

She gave a quiet laugh and busied her hands with the preparation of another cup of tea. "No, it is not Sebastian. I explained everything to him at the ball and he volunteered himself to help as well. He did not seem to consider even for a moment that he might be the subject of the letter."

"Ha!" A fork thudded against the table and every head snapped to Isabel. Her striking, green eyes had grown dark, an ache in their shadows that none of the others understood. "Gentlemen rarely realize what is in front of them."

"Well, that, we can all agree on." Felicity gave Isabel a sharp nod of approval.

With a defeated sigh, Clara poked at a slice of orange on her plate. "But that line, 'the one you seek is nearer than you think.' Who else could it mean?"

Mercy sipped her tea and hummed thoughtfully. "Isabel has a brother, as do Clara and Ellen. You know them all well enough by now."

"Please, for your sake, do not marry our brother," Clara grumbled.

"Though of course it would be wonderful to have you as our sister, Lydia," Ellen added.

The other Gardiner sister nodded quickly, a blush dusting across her cheeks made brighter by her light-red hair. "Certainly, certainly."

Once again, Lydia felt herself softening. Whoever had written that letter, whatever it really meant, she was exactly where she needed to be at this moment: surrounded by her beloved friends.

As much as she loved Isabel and the Gardiner girls, Lydia had next to nothing in common with either of their brothers. Perhaps she and her friends would discover the truth. Perhaps not. Either way, as the girls rattled off dozens of names for the identities of both Lady Swan and Lydia's gentleman, she knew these bonds would always be her foundation.

"Miss Dailey, another visitor has arrived for you."

The ladies jumped in their seats at the butler's booming announcement; they had been so lost in their increasingly improbable theories.

"Who is it?" Lydia asked. She had not been expecting anyone else today.

"Mr. Harrowsmith."

Silence filled the conservatory. Lydia's friends gave each other meaningful expressions before turning their inquisitive eyes to her. Trying her best not to acknowledge them, Lydia nodded at the butler.

The moment the doors clicked shut behind him, Lydia sent the rest of the table a warning glare. Poor Clara hid her mouth behind her napkin, already struggling to contain her excitement.

"Ah, excellent! You are all here," Sebastian called as he strode into the room behind the butler, hair windswept from the walk.

"What brings you here today, Sebastian?" Lydia asked, painfully aware of the other girls' eyes on her as she rose from her chair and met him halfway.

"Once again, I see I have been left out of your womanly secrets." The gentleman chuckled as he took in their mostly cleared plates.

"Not this time. We have all just been discussing a certain letter," Felicity offered.

Sebastian smiled wide, some unfamiliar emotion flickering in his eyes for the briefest moment. "And have you made any promising discoveries?"

Hadn't Lydia seen that same look on his face the night of the ball? Or had this matchmaker business caused her to see things that were not truly there? In any case, Lydia could hardly ask about it now with her friends already abuzz with the possibility of Sebastian.

"We will not bore you with all that nonsense," Lydia hurried to say. "Besides, we have made no more progress than you and I did the other night."

"I am sure you will with six bright minds on the task." Sebastian returned his attention to Lydia, a wavy, black lock falling across his forehead.

A sudden urge to carefully brush it back into place gripped

Lydia's chest, her fingers twitching at her sides, the only sign that anything was amiss. She knew by now how stubborn his hair could be against any and all attempts to tame it, rendering both the urge and the effort useless.

"Would you like to join my family for a picnic at Hyde Park tomorrow?" Sebastian asked, his gaze locked on Lydia before turning his inviting smile to the rest of the room.

"I am afraid my day is quite spoken for—"

"—and you will not believe whom Mother wants me to meet—"

"Tomorrow? Any day but tomorrow!"

"Busy, busy!"

"—urgent dress fitting—"

All the ladies' conflicting plans spilled forth, overlapping and drowning each other out. Sebastian jerked back, eyes blinking rapidly.

"Goodness, I knew you ladies endured overwhelming schedules during the Season, but I did not realize the severity of the problem." He laughed, the sound chiming through the large, glass room. Rounding on Lydia, Sebastian tilted his head to one side, the corner of his mouth pulled up.

Lydia looked away, pretending to ponder tomorrow's activities. "If I recall correctly, Mother has already planned on parading me about Hyde Park tomorrow. I am sure she will not object."

"Thank goodness." He sighed. "If I had returned home without any acceptances, Mama may have sent for a physician to discover what dreadful ailment has stolen my charm."

"That *dreadful ailment* would be Society's insistence on ladies spending their every waking moment attracting a spouse," Felicity mumbled, dunking a chocolate biscuit in her tea.

Sebastian nodded. "I have heard that Lady Eldmar is extremely eager to plan another wedding. I do not envy you her diligent attentions."

"That is one way to phrase it," Mercy and Felicity agreed in unison.

After a round of farewells and Sebastian's assurances to join them for the next picnic, Lydia once again found herself the sole center of attention. Her friends stared at her with confident smiles.

"Lydia, *of course* Lady Swan means Mr. Harrowsmith! I am more certain than ever!" Clara squealed, crushing her napkin in her hands, eyes aglow.

"You had convinced me otherwise earlier, but now I am inclined to agree with Clara again," Isabel mumbled more to herself than to anyone else, her gaze far away. Lydia could almost see the possibilities being studied in her friend's mind.

"He does look at you so sweetly," agreed Ellen.

Lydia huffed and settled herself back into her chair. "Sebastian looks at everyone like that. He cannot help that smile…even when he should."

"And there is the other matter." Mercy flourished a hand at Lydia. "You call him by his Christian name. None of the rest of us do and we have known him nearly as long as you."

Irritation raced up Lydia's spine with a chill. "That is only because we spent more time together as children. Our estates share a border and our parents are friends. It stands to reason that we should appear closer."

Mercy fixed Lydia with a piercing stare and leaned forward against the table. "You do not *appear* closer. You *are* closer."

Teeth and fists clenched, Lydia forced a calming inhale. "My friends, I can assure you that Sebastian is no more involved in Lady Swan's letter than any of you. It was the very first thread I followed and I immediately came to its end. Please, shall we leave it at that now?" She finished with a firm nod, prim curls bouncing.

She meant it as much for them as for herself. Seeing Sebastian today had not helped. Now that she had been made aware of it, she could not stop combing through her memory for possible reinterpretations of even the most innocuous glances and actions. Doing the same with him standing mere feet before her put Lydia in a strange mood, her head and heart dizzy by turns.

If she planned to see what she could make of Lady Swan's annoyingly vague suggestions, Lydia could not afford to distract herself by seeing signs where they did not belong.

Even if a minuscule part of her had come to find the idea of Sebastian being the answer…not entirely undesirable.

# CHAPTER SEVEN

SPRING SUNLIGHT BATHED the expansive lawn bordering the Serpentine River in a warm glow. Though he normally sought fresh air and the sun at every opportunity, today, Sebastian found it frustrating. It blinded him in the direction he was looking.

"Mr. Harrowsmith, come enjoy the shade! Surely, you will be more comfortable under here," an older woman called from the protection of the canopy behind him. "Your son has grown into a fine young man, Mrs. Harrowsmith."

"He provides an excellent example for Peter and Anthony," Mama cooed, her voice laced with pride. "Though at their age and with fewer responsibilities, accompanying their mama on a picnic did not suit their interests today."

A breeze whistled in his ears as he turned around, offering a smile to the matrons. Mama sat in the middle, her friends on each side, their children and grandchildren of varying ages chatting and playing on the blanket spread beneath the canopy or out on the grass.

"I am afraid I have been inattentive to our guests," Sebastian said with a rueful smile, ducking into the cool shadows.

As the ladies began to protest, he settled himself down onto the blanket amidst a tapestry of dolls and toy soldiers and children with chubby-cheeked smiles happy to have another playmate. Mama and her friends sighed as Sebastian enthusiastically played doctor to every toy Mrs. Chaplin's youngest child and Lady Farworth's grandchildren shoved at him. It took his mind off his tense muscles and unsettled stomach. He also knew that it made Mama proud to display her loyal, capable son who could still one day inherit his uncle's estate and title—a double blessing for her.

"And here is your dear Miss Lady, cured of a frightful bout of The Tickles," Sebastian announced, reverently revealing the doll cradled in his hands before Mrs. Chaplin's delighted little girl.

"I see you have finally made acquaintances of your own age," a familiar voice teased from somewhere behind Sebastian.

"The Dailey family is here! How good of you to join us!" Mama and her friends rose from their chairs at the edge of the blanket and braved the sunlight to greet the new arrivals.

Lydia stood just on the outside of the canopy, wearing a soft-green walking dress, light outlining her figure. Despite the bonnet shading her face, Sebastian could see the faint impression of Lydia's smile. It was not until he had reached the age of five-and-ten or so that he realized it had been there so often that he'd begun to recognize it when everyone else saw stone.

The older ladies stole her attention for a moment to hear summaries of Lydia's Season thus far before retreating to the comfort of the canopy with Mrs. Dailey. Mr. Dailey and Mr. Edmund joined the other gentlemen in attendance. Instead of taking her place amongst the other misses leisurely pacing up and down the Serpentine's curves, always within eyesight of their guardians, Lydia slipped under the awning.

"Please, do not let me interrupt," Lydia insisted. She waved a hand toward Sebastian and his toddling companions as she took an empty chair at a small table and selected a pastry from the gleaming, silver tray in the middle.

With a playful groan, Sebastian pushed himself up from the blanket. "Children, I am afraid the physician has had a very long day and must retire."

For dramatic effect, he placed a hand on his lower back and pretended to hobble toward the chair nearest Lydia. The young ones laughed, either at Sebastian's relative old age or his superb acting.

Lydia's smile widened just a touch behind her teacup. If the rest of her was stone, that smile was a feather—sometimes so fleeting, it was nearly impossible to see, sometimes lingering on her features, almost always drifting across Sebastian's memory.

The angle of Lydia's bonnet prevented Sebastian from seeing it any longer once he'd settled in his chair. A shame or a blessing, he could not determine.

"How are—"

"Kiss! Dr. Smith, kiss!"

The sudden chorus of children interrupted Sebastian's question. Anxiety flooded his senses, stomach flipping inside out, while Lydia politely choked on her tea. The children stared at them with expectant smiles.

"Why are they shouting that at you?" Lydia hissed in a whisper. A tendon twitched in her neck.

She glanced from the matrons, who seemed to think nothing of the strange imaginations and play habits of their little ones, at the opposite end of the canopy to Sebastian, her gaze lingering on Mrs. Dailey's rigid profile. Eyes wide and mouth ajar, Sebastian had gone quite speechless. Children and their strange ideas...and the strange ideas they gave him.

"Dr. Smith, kiss!" One of the boys, Lady Farworth's grandson, broke away from the pack and trotted to Sebastian, galloping his stuffed pony in the air. He crashed it into Sebastian's lap with a shrill neigh.

"Dear Master Jonathan," Sebastian said with an awkward chuckle as he patted the boy's head, "I am afraid that is not appropriate—"

A light hand gripped his forearm. "I think," Lydia started, hiding her mouth behind a gloved hand, "I think he meant he wishes for you to kiss his toy. Not—"

"Of course!" A strange mixture of relief and disappointment untwisted the anxiety coiled around Sebastian's chest. Beaming down at Master Jonathan, he gently took the worn pony and held it up before his eyes. "I cannot leave my patients behind without their remedies. Come, line up to receive your healing kisses!"

The children did just that, each eagerly waiting for Dr. Smith—"Harrowsmith" had been too lengthy for the youngest ones to say—to bestow their beloved toys with the prescribed peck. All save one. Mrs. Chaplin's daughter approached, dragging her doll behind her. Her round eyes stared up at Lydia, curious.

"Would you please kiss Miss Lady?" she asked quietly, doing her best to offer up the doll that was almost as big as her.

Taken aback, Lydia's eyes widened to match the girl's as she looked to Sebastian for some sort of assistance. He managed to school his eager smile into a smirk, paired with an unhelpful shrug. No, he would not help Lydia out of this. In fact, he rather looked forward to it.

"V-Very well," Lydia squeaked. She glanced to the older ladies fanning themselves at the other end of the long blanket and adjusted herself in her chair to block as much of their view as possible.

Sebastian noted Mrs. Dailey's position, seated in her usual place beside his mother and keeping her quite engaged in conversation. If it were not for the immense and unfair burdens she forced Lydia to endure, he might have thanked her for the kindness she did Mama in maintaining their closeness over the years.

"Hurry," little Miss Chaplin whined, sending a panicked glance over her shoulder as her friends raced each other into the sunlight.

Attention back on Lydia, Sebastian realized that she still sat frozen, staring at the child with a tenderness in her eyes that made his heart hum. He leaned to one side, bumping her shoulder with his. "Go on. Miss Lady awaits."

Lydia glared icy daggers into him for a flash of a moment, as if this were somehow his fault. Sebastian fought the urge to laugh as she put on quite a show of bracing herself for a little playacting, sitting up taller, bringing her shoulders back, lifting her chin proudly into the air, her hair a rich brown in the shade. At the very least, he knew he should commend the dignity Lydia gave to every action, no matter how menial or seemingly demeaning.

A hand sliced through the air, palm up. "Very well," Lydia repeated, this time with confidence.

The girl gave her doll one last hug before gingerly placing it in Lydia's care, an expectant smile spreading from cheek to chubby cheek. "Thank you, Miss Dailey," she half-whispered, half-giggled behind a tiny fist. The lovely dear's manners were already forming well by the tender age of three.

The older miss, no doubt aware of her opportunity to model perfect ladylike behavior on a receptive young mind, sat so precisely on the edge of her chair that Sebastian thought she must have been floating. Lydia's grace made everything she did seem like floating. Whether natural or practiced or a combination of the two, it mattered not to him. He could not help admiring everything Lydia did, everything she was.

The picture of elegance, Lydia held up the doll and lowered her head, keeping her neck long and straight. She planted a chaste kiss amongst the doll's red, yarn hair, lips pressed together rather than puckered. "There," she announced, straightening up immediately and thrusting the toy back to Mrs. Chaplin's daughter.

"Very well done," Sebastian offered, quietly clapping as Miss Chaplin skipped out onto the grass happily, dragging her precious doll behind her.

"Oh, hush," Lydia snipped, waving a hand through the air as if dispelling an irritating insect.

"No, it was very well done," he insisted. "Look. You made that girl exceedingly happy."

Lydia's eyes followed his. They watched Miss Chaplin spin around with Miss Lady, laughing with the simple delight of childhood.

Sebastian could feel rather than see Lydia's peaceful smile.

The hum in his heart increased in intensity, as if longing to rise to the occasion, to do whatever it took to see that contented expression every single day. He knew she desired children. Nearly every woman did, if only to secure their family's fortunes and reputations for another generation. Those women did not look at children like Lydia did.

"Mother would reproach me for being silly." Lydia spoke so quietly, Sebastian almost missed it. "At least, she preferred to leave the play and laughter to our nannies and governesses." Though she lowered her head once more, Lydia's eyes remained fixed on Mrs. Dailey.

Sebastian gave a sympathetic nod. Something squeezed his chest, bitter and aching. In truth, Lydia had not been raised much differently than most children of the *ton*. Their parents had the means to employ others to look after their children. Still, Mrs. Dailey operated her motherly role with a particularly severe chill that would no doubt cause anxieties and insecurities in any child.

"You do not have to do the same, you know," Sebastian whispered. He did his best to shove his own inconsequential suffering back into the depths where they belonged. He had always known that he would not be the one to fulfill this dream for her.

When Lydia's head snapped to him, he offered a small smile that he hoped spoke only of his support for a friend and nothing of that unwelcome smolder of deep, sympathetic pain that could only have one foundation.

"Mother never made it seem possible that another option should exist. Engaging in child's play is beneath the dignity of a proper lady."

Sebastian's smile tightened. "Because the existence of another option means your mother would have to admit the possibility of being incorrect."

To his surprise, Lydia bit her bottom lip, fighting a smile of her own. "Now, *that* is a sight I would not mind witnessing just once in my life."

A laugh burst from Sebastian, drawing the attention of every person under the canopy and within its vicinity. The ensuing slap to the shoulder from Lydia arrived precisely on time. The smile he saw, the way Lydia's eyes had turned into happy crescents, made it worth it.

"Lydia dearest," Mrs. Dailey called, her voice as sharp as her gaze. "Is something the matter?"

Every spark of joy and amusement evaporated in an instant. The marble returned. "No, Mother, not at all. I was merely frightened by an insect."

Mrs. Dailey kept her daughter pinned in place for another long moment. Judging, perhaps, or choosing which criticisms to spew later.

"You know, that is the dreadful thing about spending time out of doors. The fresh air and sunlight do wonders for the body and spirit and yet…the insects!" Mama lamented.

The other women offered their hearty agreement. Mrs. Dailey returned her attention to the hostess, remembering her greater obligation, and released Lydia from her grasp.

"Deftly maneuvered, my friend," Sebastian said, lowering his head in a respectful bow. "But you and I both know that you would sooner be offended by an insect than frightened."

This time, Lydia did not attempt to hide her smile. "Respectable ladies are meant to be frightened by, well, almost anything within reason. You are in possession of privileged information, Sebastian."

Within reason. What an interesting idea, Sebastian thought to himself. He should become acquainted with it.

Now was not the time, not with the way Lydia's eyes glimmered, their shared secrets protected under blue depths. In truth, Lydia was right. Sebastian did possess privileged information. He had spent a lifetime learning to recognize and witness the heart and passion in his best friend, both tender and bold by turns. If Society's bachelors ever saw that, Lady Swan would be forced to set her sights upon another lady in need or else retire her quill altogether.

Lady Swan. Lydia's matchmaker. Sebastian's limbs grew heavy. It had been pleasant to forget about that business for a while—to forget the fact that if he had not crossed Lydia's mind as a possibility by now, he never would.

"On the topic of privileged information…" Sebastian forced out with a chuckle, suddenly parched, and focused his attention on pouring himself a cup of tea. "Have you and our friends had any success with a certain mystery?"

"Not in the least, I am afraid," Lydia replied quickly, almost before Sebastian had finished his question. Tilting his head back to take a long sip, he eyed the lady from his peripheral vision. Her own cup could not hide the hint of a blush on Lydia's sharp cheekbones.

Why should she be more embarrassed by it now than she'd been when she had first told him at Lady Spurgold's welcome ball? Sebastian could only think of one reason.

"It is still early in the Season, darling Lydia," he said quietly, forcing his own interests to the back of his mind. They had been escaping to the forefront far too often of late.

"Leaving already?" The worry in Mama's voice caught Sebastian's attention. He looked across to the other end of the blanket to find Mrs. Chaplin offering her apologies and farewells.

Lydia noticed as well. Without another word to Sebastian, she passed her cup to a nearby footman and crossed to the group of older women. Sebastian watched as she said goodbye to Mrs. Chaplin, little Miss Chaplin, and Miss Lady, then took the now-vacant seat beside his mother.

Lydia knew of Mama's dislike of leaving any chair beside her empty, a chair that would have been occupied by Papa. Yet somehow, without Sebastian saying a word of it today, she instinctively knew what the widow needed and had immediately sought to fill a vacancy.

Easing back into his chair, Sebastian watched the ladies as he absentmindedly munched on a raspberry tart. When Mama rubbed her bare arms and commented on the chill breeze, Lydia was the first to reach for a shawl. She even tucked in the extra fabric between the small of Mama's back and the chair, creating a comfortable cushion. The younger lady listened to every story and offered insightful comments or asked interested questions. How had no one noticed these touches of care beneath the aloof facade?

Sebastian's heart lurched when Mama smiled and grasped one of Lydia's hands in both of hers with apparent gratitude. They already admired each other like family. Surely, the idea of Lydia becoming family one day did not seem that far-fetched. Perhaps it had not seemed so to everyone else. It should not have to him.

A tingle raced down Sebastian's spine. His eyes snapped up to find Lydia staring directly at him. Had she somehow peered into his thoughts? It would not be the first time, certainly. Sebastian reeled back, fear snaking through his stomach, as Lydia rose from her chair and crossed the blanket toward him.

A thousand words populated in Sebastian's throat, clogging it until he could not speak. He could only watch and wonder as Lydia stopped just before him and looked down her narrow nose at him. She *had* read his thoughts, hadn't she? Why else would she be glowering at him?

Sebastian had finally managed to pry his mouth open in an attempt to make any sound when Lydia leaned forward, dark curls springing around her face. Every muscle froze, the very *air* seemed to freeze, as lace-covered fingers daintily brushed a smattering of crumbs from his vest. He relaxed. He had not even realized he'd made such a mess.

At least it had inspired Lydia to dote on him a little. Even if it was the sort of doting tinged with reprimand. What could he say? Sebastian had grown rather fond of Lydia's particular approach to affection.

# Chapter Eight

THAT SILLY SMILE had no place on a countenance as handsome as Sebastian's. All Lydia had done was clean him up—a job that he should have been capable of himself by now. Why should he get to look so charming when he really should look mortified for making a lady exert herself?

Sebastian let out a breathy laugh. "Many thanks. You have always known how to look after me best, eh?"

Lydia swallowed, suddenly weightless. She pressed her lips together. Taking care of Sebastian was not all bad, she supposed. Not when he looked at her like that and said such pretty things.

"Lady Farworth has suggested a walk about the park. Would you care to walk with me?"

The question only hung in the air for a moment before Lydia's eyes widened. Embarrassment gnawed a pit in her stomach. "Forgive me. It is a gentleman's place to offer the invitation."

Lydia jumped as Sebastian leapt to his feet in one fluid movement. He brandished a hand before her. "Why should I mind? We are far more than just a lady and a gentleman by now. We are friends. Or has the excitement of Lady Swan's letter addled your mind that much?"

Instinctively, reflexively, Lydia took Sebastian's hand. His strong fingers curled around hers with just the right amount of pressure.

"Perhaps it has," she mumbled more to herself than him.

Lydia's absurd heart fluttered at the least important part of Sebastian's statement. They *did* transcend lady and gentleman. She had always known that, hadn't she? Since the arrival of Lady Swan's letter, the precise nature of their relationship had grown murky. At least to Lydia. Sebastian appeared none the wiser to her inner turmoil. He knew precisely where they stood. Still, that was not what mattered most.

They were friends. This was just Sebastian. He said charming, teasing things to her with numbing regularity. Now she felt *something* and she did not welcome it. Feelings rarely boded well.

"Do not lag too far behind, Lydia," Mother called, her angular beauty illuminated by the early afternoon sunlight as she walked with one arm looped around Mrs. Harrowsmith's.

"Coming, Mother," Lydia forced herself to reply.

Sebastian angled his elbow toward her, giving it an amusing flap up and down. Securing her bonnet a little tighter, Lydia managed to hide the smile she found less compelling to fight with every passing moment.

The pair followed behind the small group of older ladies clustered under parasols across the magnificently green lawn, the Serpentine glinting to their left. Lydia kept her gaze forward, thankful for the protection of the bonnet while also wishing she could catch a glimpse at Sebastian's expression.

"I must say, you are not looking as cross as usual lately," Sebastian started once they'd settled into a comfortable walking pace toward the bridge. "If you are having an enjoyable Season thus far, perhaps you did not need Lady Swan after all?"

Lydia stiffened. "Have I not been looking as cross? Goodness, I shall have to try harder. I *do* have a reputation to uphold. The Season is exactly as I have come to expect." She scoffed. "It is a long series of necessary headaches and annoyances. Yet I know my place, so I shall forge ahead."

The gentleman reached across his broad chest to pat Lydia's hand, resting atop his forearm. "It cannot be as bad as all that now that we have the mystery of this letter to solve."

Only now had Lydia begun to regret confiding in Sebastian about the whole matter. He seemed just as eager as her friends to uncover the truth, even if Lydia herself was still not entirely sure there was any truth to find. Though she had invited it upon herself, Lydia would not have minded a respite from Sebastian's frequent mentions of Lady Swan. None of them had had any strokes of brilliance regarding that identity, either, though not for lack of trying.

"It has added some...suspense to the Season," Lydia conceded. She dipped her head even lower to ensure her bonnet would not reveal the heat simmering under her skin.

"See? It is already more interesting than any of your past Seasons. Surely, that gives it an advantage."

Lydia muffled a sigh. She would only find her way out of this entanglement by telling Sebastian what he clearly longed to hear. "Yes, I suppose so."

"Ah, look there," Sebastian whispered, leaning in even closer. Lydia had no choice but to look up in the direction her friend indicated toward a gentleman and lady walking arm in arm, much like them, along a perpendicular gravel path. Neither spoke. Their expressions, though perfectly polite, lacked a certain warmth of contentment that tugged at Lydia's curiosity.

"That is Lord Rollinswell and Lady Elizabeth. He is a friend of mine from my club and she is the youngest daughter of the Earl of Belbury. Sources have informed me that they have each fallen for the other's lesser titled friend and are only courting in the open to appease their parents until she turns one-and-twenty next month."

Lydia gasped quietly, ears perked. She did enjoy the odd gossip now and again, and Sebastian always had the newest and most fascinating news. Unlike herself, he was well loved within many circles of the *ton* and acted as a confidante for his friends and acquaintances...just as he had always done with Lydia.

"Unfortunately," Sebastian continued, "my sources also inform me that Lady Elizabeth's parents have been sensing something amiss in her seemingly perfect courtship. The real couple fears they will soon need to expedite their plans."

"They would not dare go… Not to Gretna Green?" she whispered in shock. Other people's follies certainly had a way of helping one distract oneself from one's own painfully real circumstances. Unable to help herself any longer, Lydia tilted her head back to look at Sebastian unhindered by her bonnet's lacy frills.

"Indeed, to that very place where scandal breeds matrimony," Sebastian replied in a hushed tone, one brow raised conspiratorially.

He continued the story and started others, often losing himself on digressions of varying relativity. Most of the time, he managed to pick up abandoned threads of past stories and somehow find a way to wrap them all together.

Lydia listened to every word. The spring-green grass and treetops of Hyde Park melted into the background as Sebastian's voice painted his amusing and colorful tales. Clara might have been the best orator of their group of ladies, but Sebastian still remained Lydia's favorite storyteller. He infused every morsel from London's rumor mill, from the mundane to the remarkable, with enthusiasm and character.

The tension in Lydia's brows, jaw, and shoulders eased as she contentedly absorbed all of Sebastian's chatter about their surroundings and the recent goings-on of the *ton*. She finally felt at ease again, like everything had returned to normal.

This whole letter business had taken up far more of Lydia's mind and energy than she cared to admit, even to her dearest friends. It had complicated her affections for Sebastian, no doubt manipulated by the letter, whether that had been the writer's intention or not. She had needed this time away from talk of swans and solving mysteries.

Until, of course, Sebastian began rattling off names of gentlemen he had seen Lydia interact with in past Seasons, or gentlemen from his own circle he thought Lydia might tolerate.

She swallowed, unable to ease the sudden dryness in her throat.

"Careful, Lyd—"

A jarring step and a swift twist turned Lydia's world nearly upside down. "Ah!" she cried. Pain lanced up her foot as her walking boot came down on something hard and sharp, her ankle buckling.

Strong, firm hands gripping her arms steadied her. Sebastian peered down into Lydia's face, searching her. "Are you hurt?"

Heat radiated into Lydia's bare skin where Sebastian touched her. It raced to every hidden part of her, threatening to breach her heart.

"Yes, yes, I am fine," she grumbled, putting what focus she could manage into wrangling free. Mother's horrified reaction at the sight of her daughter publicly stumbling into a man's arms was a mere flicker in Lydia's mind as far as immediately pressing concerns went.

"Yes, you are fine or yes, you are hurt?" Sebastian demanded. His thumbs brushed against her skin as his eyes continued to search hers for signs of pain or injury. Heavens, why were long gloves only required at formal evening events?

"Sebastian, I am unhurt," Lydia insisted.

"You are positive?" he asked again, brows raised, disappearing under thick, black hair.

Lydia forced herself to truly consider her friend's question for a moment. Taking a deep breath, she paused, slowed her heart, and cleared her mind.

"Yes, I am sure. My ankle twisted, but if it is sprained, it is so minor, I hardly notice it now. What was the culprit?"

Sebastian nodded to the left of the gravel path, sloping down toward the banks of the river. A gray rock protruded from a tuft of swaying grass.

Mother's sharp, inquisitive cough caught their attention. She, Mrs. Harrowsmith, and another one of Mrs. Harrowsmith's friends had all paused at the crest of the bridge, staring at the pair on the bank below.

"Forgive me," Lydia called, lowering her head in a display of shame. "I turned my ankle on a rock, but no harm has been done."

*"That remains to be seen,"* said the daggers in Mother's eyes.

She shrank even further, tucking herself a little deeper into Sebastian's side. The admonishments would go flying the moment they returned to the townhouse. Lydia had breached etiquette twice in one day—at one event. That would not go unnoticed or unremarked upon.

For now, Mother only gave a single firm nod and offered gracious apologies to her friends on behalf of her bumbling daughter. The matrons continued their leisurely walk across the bridge, Mother and Mrs. Harrowsmith's friend both angling their parasols so as to appear at the best advantage for every eye in Hyde Park.

"I did try to warn you," Sebastian said with feigned disappointment, patting her hand once again. The humor returned the moment he knew Lydia was well and truly unharmed. Or perhaps he was trying to distract her from her mother's ire. Either way, Lydia welcomed it.

The gentleman offered his arm once more and Lydia accepted. She knew she always would. And she knew Sebastian was correct.

"Yes, so you did." She chuckled lightly.

He had tried to warn her when the letter had first arrived that he was not a candidate for the gentleman in question. Why had Lydia found it harder and harder to accept that truth when just a week ago, the idea of Sebastian being a prospect for her husband would have sounded utterly bizarre?

"Ah, it does feel wonderful to be correct for once." Sebastian puffed out his chest and gave Lydia one of his typical half-smiles in profile.

*Indeed,* Lydia thought to herself, *it would feel wonderful to be correct for once.*

# CHAPTER NINE

As THE ABBOTT family's butler announced the arrival of the Harrowsmiths, Sebastian's eyes swept over the handsome drawing room for the one face he always sought first. Disappointment twinged in his stomach when he failed to spot Lydia on the sofa or on one of the armchairs or by the simmering fireplace or the glass display of Mr. Abbott's pocket watch collection, which she had no doubt seen a hundred times already.

"Ah, Mr. Harrowsmith."

Sebastian turned to his left to find Lady Ainsworth, Miss Abbott's aunt and chaperone since Mrs. Abbott's passing.

"Lady Ainsworth, how are you this evening?" Sebastian bowed to the older woman. Mama and his younger brothers offered their greetings to the lady and dispersed throughout the room in search of acquaintances.

"Very well indeed, thank you. My dear niece Isabel charged me with ensuring you did not wander away should you arrive before she returned," Lady Ainsworth continued, slow and calm as always. "Something about needing to discuss certain matters with you."

Sebastian's eyes widened, embarrassment flaming across every inch of skin. As embroiled as he felt in Lady Swan's scheme, he had no interest in discussing it with the sensible parental figures in their lives. "A-And that did not spark any curiosity in you, my lady?"

The dowager countess gracefully hid her smile behind a gloved hand, fine lines appearing at the corners of her wise eyes.

"No, no." She laughed, swishing her hand to dispel the idea. "I remember my own days of the youthful little secrets that were precious to me. I shall let you all keep yours—so long as they will not ruin reputations." Lady Ainsworth lifted a warning brow.

Cool relief combatted the scorch of Sebastian's anxiety. He laughed and held up both hands. "Not at all. I do not think any of us have the interest nor time nor resources to court true scandal."

Lady Ainsworth rested a hand over her heart. "That is just what every loving aunt longs to hear."

"Mr. Harrowsmith!"

Sebastian and the countess looked over his shoulder. Miss Abbott stood in the doorway just behind them. "Thank you, Aunt Matilda," she said to Lady Ainsworth with a polite nod.

"I take that to mean I am dismissed." Lady Ainsworth chuckled as she melted away into a nearby cluster of guests.

"This letter," Miss Abbott started, keeping her voice low. She gestured for Sebastian to follow her toward a quieter corner of the drawing room.

"Yes, I thought your request to speak with me might have something to do with that," Sebastian said, wearing a rueful smile.

"Well, what theories do you have?"

"I am afraid to say I truly have none."

"Truly?" Miss Abbott narrowed her eyes. She had always been the most studious and analytical of the Bainbridge ladies. "You see, I have taken to dissecting each line for hidden meaning. A puzzle or a code, perhaps."

Sebastian could not help laughing quietly at his friend's enthusiasm. "Lady Swan is already cryptic enough, and now there are puzzles?"

Miss Abbott frowned thoughtfully. "When it comes to a letter of mysterious origin, one cannot rule out a single possibility. I have already transcribed it from memory and read it backward, so

I have ruled that one out."

"Perhaps try marking every other letter to see if it spells anything," Sebastian suggested.

He did his best to humor her as more dinner guests filtered in for the usual preliminary drawing room mingle. He had also managed to angle himself with a view of the door. Still no Lydia.

"Mr. Harrowsmith, is that you?" called a high, lilting voice.

The ever-present knot of apprehension and anticipation in Sebastian's stomach twisted. Miss Woods was here. He forced a smile, ignoring Miss Abbott's curious expression, and turned.

Miss Woods's smile spread from one rosy, round cheek to the other, sandy-brown hair curled to frame her heart-shaped face. An icy fist clenched around Sebastian's chest, an unfortunately familiar sensation. He hated to see a lady look at him like this. It would never end how they wanted, yet he could only do so much to dissuade them short of openly rejecting them.

It would be the height of ungentlemanly conduct unless his affections were already engaged. As far as the rest of the *ton* could see, Sebastian's affections had no claim upon them. Thus, he found himself repeatedly in this uncomfortable situation until another man managed to turn the lady's head.

"Good evening, Miss Woods. How wonderful to see you here so unexpectedly," Sebastian offered. Indeed, if he had known the Abbotts would be inviting Miss Woods and her family, he might have found himself burdened with prior commitments.

"It is entirely too wonderful to see you tonight, Mr. Harrowsmith." Miss Woods sighed, hopes of romance and matrimony glinting in her large eyes.

At least Miss Abbott joined their conversation, taking some of Miss Woods's focus away from Sebastian. Until the Misses Reeve arrived and pulled Miss Abbott away. As if sensing his loss of defense, two more young ladies Sebastian had met at other events excused themselves from their current conversations to join Sebastian's. If Miss Woods minded their addition, she kept such feelings neatly tucked away behind her genteel training.

As the minutes dragged by and Sebastian's new companions continued to block his view of the door with the feathers and flashing jewels in their hair, his discomfort became an itch, so unbearable, it could make one act out in the strangest ways for a mere moment of relief. The ladies chattered away at him, asking overlapping questions without giving him an opportunity to answer, which was preferable to Sebastian. It saved him from blurting out some nonsense just to escape.

"Mr. Harrowsmith, I am curious. Has anyone captured your particular regard this Season?"

Sebastian's throat closed. Naturally, Miss Woods had been the one to ask that unwanted question. Heat rushed up the back of his neck as his mind spun in search of any excuse.

"I wonder, is that a painting by Mr. Abel Euston?"

That most familiar of voices came at the most desperate moment. He only had a split second to act, leaning toward the other question just in time to pretend he had not heard Miss Woods's.

Blessed, beautiful Lydia stood mere feet away to his left, hands clasped behind her back, as she gazed inquisitively at the large painting of an ancient castle occupying the opposite wall. Sebastian had been so distracted by the ladies vying for his attention that he had not seen or heard Lydia's family arrive.

"Forgive me, ladies, but would you mind if I excused myself? I am quite familiar with Mr. Euston's work, you see," Sebastian said with an apologetic frown that had somehow earned him more favor with at least two of the ladies based on how they fluttered their eyelashes and nodded along. The others seemed disappointed but not entirely disheartened. The night was young, after all.

When Sebastian reached Lydia, he let out a long, much-needed exhale. For added comedic effect for his own sake, he tugged at the starched collar of his crisp, white dinner shirt.

"Oh, stop that," Lydia chided from the corner of her mouth, gently swatting at Sebastian's hand. "They would be hurt if they saw you."

"Yes, yes, you are right," Sebastian hastily agreed, guilt prickling in his stomach.

"Of course I am."

A trace of laughter lingered under the surface of Lydia's words. Sebastian dared a glance. His friend watched him from the corner of her eye, a small smile lighting her entire face. It was the perfect jewel to complement all the others sparkling in her curls, dangling from her ears, draped around her neck, and threaded into the fine, spring-green fabric of her evening gown.

"You did not look like you would survive until dinner, so I thought I should rescue you," Lydia explained, fighting a giggle that Sebastian so longed to hear loud and free.

A smile slowly spread across Sebastian's features as he shook his head. "Thank the heavens you did. I am eternally in your debt, dearest Lydia."

She was clever and quick on her feet, indeed. Sebastian had always admired those traits. This was certainly not the first time they had benefited him or come to his aid in some way, and certainly would not be the last. Sebastian could hardly fathom life without them—without *her*—by his side, providing safe haven, companionship—

"So, you say you are an expert on Mr. Euston over there," Lydia continued, nodding toward the grand painting, a well-known work of her own recommendation.

Several years ago, when they'd taken up this townhouse, Miss Abbott and her father had reached an impasse on what type of painting should be the focal point of their new drawing room. In the end, after a game of whist, Mr. Abbott had won his preference of a castle over Miss Abbott's floral piece.

To Miss Abbott's greater frustration, Mr. Abbott had eventually come to the conclusion that he was not particular about the exact artwork chosen. Instead, he had deferred to his daughter once again, who had then deferred to Lydia's particularly expensive knowledge of fine paintings. Naturally, Lydia had seized the opportunity to recommend her favorite artist, who excelled at Mr. Abbott's preferred style.

"I did not say I was an expert. I said I was quite familiar," Sebastian corrected her as he, too, admired the stunning painting, the quality and detail of the castle's every stone evident wherever the eye landed.

He had never applied more effort than was necessary to learn the important artists of past and present, yet he had come to develop a fondness for Mr. Euston's works. Sebastian sometimes struggled to glean the same depth or meaning as others in the field of artistic interpretation, yet he could always see what drew Lydia to a piece of Mr. Euston's.

"One might assume that those two terms are synonymous," Lydia countered, absentmindedly tilting her head to one side, eyes tracing the castle's regal towers. Her peridot and diamond necklace adjusted against the exposed skin of her neck.

"Only you would assume that, Lydia." Sebastian chuckled, forcing his eyes back to the painting.

"And did I assume correctly that you were overwhelmed by the attention afforded one of the most eligible bachelors of the *ton*?"

Sebastian shook his head again, this time earnestly. "You exaggerate. My mother has thoughtfully reminded all her friends that her son remains unmarried; in line for a barony, as far as anyone yet knows; and still reasonably handsome—so she says."

"She is correct on all counts," Lydia stated matter-of-factly.

"All counts? Is that so?" Sebastian mused, pinching his chin between thumb and forefinger.

Lydia exhaled an exasperated sigh. "I would not allow that to overly inflate your sense of self-importance. Young ladies would struggle to throw themselves upon the good graces of…notably older or less physically appealing men, no matter the vast wealth or enviable title to be gained. That is simply the way of fickle human attraction."

"Ah, so it is only fickle, their interest in me. Purely superficial," Sebastian pressed, clasping his hands behind his back. "It has nothing to do with the possibility that I might be charming? Or interesting, perhaps? Thoughtful, even?"

Lydia did her best to appear intimidating to Sebastian without giving the same impression to the other dinner guests—a challenge she somehow managed to surpass. "You always try to find a cunning way to twist my words into your own meaning," she grumbled. Her bottom lip flashed out in a pout, gone in an instant, returned to its trained neutral line.

"So you do find me charming, interesting, and thoughtful?" Sebastian gasped in exaggerated surprise. Every inch of him hummed with the delight of their natural, effortless banter.

Shaking her head to hide her burgeoning smile, Lydia reached across the narrow gap between them and pinched Sebastian's forearm. He stifled a real gasp this time. She used to pinch his arm—or wherever she could best reach, depending on the predicament—whenever Sebastian had needed a reminder of manners. As they had grown older, it had transformed into a sort of teasing. Until, of course, Mrs. Dailey had noticed and put an end to yet another harmless expression of love between Lydia and the people she cared for.

At present, Sebastian could not remember the last time either of them had used it. It felt so familiar, an instantaneous reminder of their shared childhood. This time, it was also fresh, exciting, exhilarating, a promise of something Sebastian wanted so badly, something that did not seem so far-fetched in moments like these.

It was an impossible feeling, one Sebastian should not want and one he could not release. Not with Lydia looking at him with such charmingly imploring eyes, a hand outstretched for him and him alone.

"Sebastian, are you coming?" Lydia whispered, leaning closer and glancing over her shoulder.

The rest of the world rushed back into Sebastian's awareness. The scattered conversation had begun to filter toward the double doors on the other end of the drawing room, the dining room and their meal just beyond. He could only nod and accept Lydia's hand, threading her arm around his to escort her.

"I pray that Isabel has influenced the seating arrangements in your favor," Lydia said quietly as they fell into place at the end of the line of couples.

"And what such seating arrangement would that be?" Sebastian whispered back.

Lydia peered up at him wearing an incredulous frown. "Why, me beside you, of course."

"Of course," Sebastian agreed, trying and failing to swallow the lump that had suddenly become lodged in his throat.

"Otherwise, you will be left to fend for yourself amongst the other unmarried ladies in attendance, one seated on each side. Or is that desirable to you now after all my nagging? Surely, they will be more inclined to turn a blind eye to your missteps."

"Never." Sebastian scoffed. "You keep me on the right path."

Lydia did keep him on the right path, but Sebastian had always assumed it was one ultimately separate from hers. As the new Season wore on, it became increasingly difficult for him to fend off the desire to create a shared path with her. When they quipped back and forth so freely and understood each other instinctively as they did tonight, as if no one else existed or mattered, it felt so natural that Sebastian found himself longing to embrace the warm invitation of that idea…for once.

"Then maneuver us to the left a bit," Lydia instructed as they emerged into the brightly lit dining room. Sebastian gladly followed as his friend led them around the long table to their seats, side by side.

"THANK YOU FOR gracing our dinner with your presences, my lovely friends," Isabel said, arms spread wide, as she followed Lydia, Mercy, and Felicity to the doors of the drawing room, their families already halfway down the stairs. "Mercy, see what you can discover about that gentleman at your brother's club. It is not the strongest possibility, but it is the only one we have had since—"

"Yes, but I do not want you putting any strain on yourself, Mercy," Lydia insisted. She forced her eyes back to her friends. Since dinner had ended and everyone had returned to the drawing room for more conversation, her attention had wandered too often to the group of ladies by the fireplace. Sebastian, a head taller than most of them, stood at its center. At least this time, he had Edmund and one of his London friends with whom to share the women's eager attention.

"That goes for all of you, and I shall repeat the same to Ellen and Clara, if only they had not left so early," Lydia continued. "You all have your own Seasons to manage. I can manage mine as well. The letter is nothing more than an amusing pastime."

Her friends grumbled about Lydia preventing them from helping the entire way down the stairs. She ignored their pleas, head held high, and offered them and their families farewells in the Abbotts' foyer. On the carriage ride home, Mother busied herself with lecturing Edmund for his lively, stubborn philosophical debate with Mr. Abbott while Father attempted to doze, arms crossed over his chest. All else faded as Lydia let the dark streets of London on the other side of the window blur into memories of the evening.

How could everything seem so normal between her and Sebastian with this strange, unspoken undercurrent tethering them together now?

And of course, she had done *that*. The pinch, their childhood signal that had kept Sebastian out of trouble with their mothers and governesses. He hadn't seemed to mind it. In fact, he'd seemed rather amused that Lydia had revived that old thing. A touch of pride glimmered inside her. She appreciated any chance she had to amuse Sebastian since he was the one always amusing her.

"Welcome home," their London butler called as the driver and footmen rushed to help the family down from the carriage.

Lydia blinked her eyes rapidly. Their townhouse rose several stories into the twinkling night sky, dark save for a few candlelit windows. Home already. She barely remembered the ride for all her girlish woolgathering.

With home in sight, fatigue settled on Lydia's limbs like a heavy down blanket. When had dinner parties become so tiring? When all her friends wanted to badger her about mysterious matchmaking plots, apparently. When fighting thoughts of a particular friend and trying to puzzle out why her heart beat so erratically preoccupied half her energy. The other half she spent on appearing as normal as possible.

The absolute last thing Lydia wanted—her most dreaded outcome—was for Sebastian to feel pressured by her own confused feelings to admit affections that did not truly belong to him, to fit the fanciful storyline set forth by Lady Swan's letter.

Exhaustion set in as Lydia bid goodnight to her parents and brother at the end of the hall. She forced her weary body and mind to claw through the last few feet to her own room as if swimming through mud. She did not know how she would survive the rest of the Season at this rate.

As soon as Lydia's door had clicked closed behind her, she pressed her back to it and let her head fall against it, diamonds clinking against wood. She silently prayed for a good night's sleep. If she remained fully rested, she could handle anything else. Unfortunately, more often than not since the Season's strange beginning, sleep had eluded Lydia.

Her eyes opened and landed on a small, rectangular shadow on the center of her bed. Amazement surged through Lydia. She stood frozen in place. It must have been from Lady Swan. Of course it must have. What other letter would arrive by such mysterious means?

Picking up her candle from the edge of her writing desk with one hand, Lydia gathered her skirts with the other and rushed across the room. She grabbed the folded sheet of paper, balanced on the corner of her bed, and set the candle on the nightstand, all in one fluid motion.

Lydia took a deep breath. The handwriting on the front, now painfully familiar after dozens of rereads, matched. On the underside of the letter, she ran her fingertips over the wax seal's grooves and lumps. She could not determine its shape by touch alone. If she wanted to confirm her suspicions, she would have to turn it over.

A dark-purple swan leapt from the bland page, its long neck curved elegantly. Lydia's eyes widened to the size of dinner plates. Her stomach flipped and twisted and threatened to fall to her feet and shoot through her mouth at the same time. Was it a positive sign or an ill omen?

The seal popped open easily and Lydia unfolded the letter, her fingers cold and clumsy. The angle of the candlelight cast too many shadows over the anonymous writer's words, forcing Lydia to crouch beneath the flickering fire.

Both eager and terrified, Lydia skimmed the letter first. The second time, she forced herself to read slower, to absorb its contents. The third time, her attention went directly to the middle portion—her next quest.

*"It is often most difficult to accurately judge ourselves, Miss Dailey, for better or worse. You may not feel as though you are progressing on your bold undertaking, but allow this humble observer to assure you that progress is happening—even when you cannot see it. Perhaps especially then.*

*"Reveal the child in you, the child who needs love, and the right one will rise to meet that need and adore you all the more for it."*

# CHAPTER TEN

LAUGHTER SPILLED FROM the Harrowsmiths' card room as the butler announced the Daileys' arrival. It made Mother's nose wrinkle in distaste. Though she enjoyed spending time with her old friend Mrs. Harrowsmith, having both arrived in Bainbridge together as young brides around the same time, Mother usually found these informal gatherings a touch too boisterous for her stiff sensibilities despite the fact that the guest list consisted entirely of their trusted Bainbridge friends.

"Just in time!" Clara cheered from a nearby round table. "We need another for whist if you would like to join us." She waved to Lydia, lively as always.

Mother nodded her permission to Lydia and drifted across the room toward the hostess and the other matrons. Feeling a little looser now that Mother had her distraction and Father and Edmund had spotted Lord Eldmar and Mr. Abbott, Lydia settled into the chair beside her friend.

"Wonderful!" Clara bounced in her seat and clasped Lydia's hands in hers. "Felicity will be joining as well."

"May I request the honor of being your partner, Lydia?"

Lydia's entire body tingled at the sound of Sebastian's voice behind her.

"No, Uncle Sebastian! Whist is boring!"

Both Sebastian and Lydia peered behind him to see his two young nieces sprawled on the rug in the middle of the room with all manner of toys scattered about them. The older girl crossed her arms over her chest and glowered to the best of her ability, the effect undermined by her own round cheeks and charming pout.

"Miss Dorothy, I was just wondering if you would show me your enthralling play," Isabel suggested, leaping up from her chess match with her younger brother, shushing his complaints. She joined the girls on the rug, turning her encouraging smile to each of them. "I saw bits and pieces just now and I must say I am utterly captivated. Perhaps you and little Miss Christina could act it out for me first, and then your uncle can rejoin you."

"You can watch our play!" the girl cried, dancing a full circle around Isabel before settling back down behind her toy theater. Sebastian's younger niece, just two years old, contentedly waved her stiff arms in the air and waddled back and forth across Isabel's view.

"So you are free to join us, then, Mr. Harrowsmith?" Felicity asked, appearing behind Sebastian and taking her seat, as if the pairs had already been established.

"I suppose I am—if Lydia will grant my request."

Lydia returned her gaze to the table and waved a hand. "Of course. You know you are my favorite whist partner. Not dramatic—" She paused and nodded toward Clara, who giggled behind her hand. "And not quick to temper." This time, she nodded to Felicity.

"Did you hear that, Clara?" The older Reeve twin glanced between Lydia and Sebastian wearing a smug smirk. "Look closely, all! Lydia has just made an eternal whist enemy. It is now my personal mission to defeat you at every opportunity. And Clara here shall help me claim my first victory."

Felicity slapped the unsuspecting girl between the shoulder blades. Clara yelped and clamped both hands over her mouth. "I will?" she whispered from between her fingers.

"Do not listen to her, dear," Lydia insisted, knowingly rising to Felicity's bait. They were two of the most competitive in their group. "Sebastian and I will soon free you from the torment of being Felicity's partner."

"Are you just as confident in your prospects, Mr. Harrowsmith?" Felicity turned her nose up toward Sebastian, bold and challenging.

The gentleman held up both hands and quickly settled into his seat. "I gain my confidence from Lydia's. I am merely here to support." He grinned at Lydia.

The earnestness in his words and shining eyes nearly melted her into a puddle. But Lydia would not allow that to stop her from defeating Felicity.

Somehow, Sebastian's eyes still shone despite losing. He had laughed all along the way, whether they'd had a good turn or a bad one. It was one of the traits in Sebastian that Lydia found herself most envious of—the ability to navigate through life's difficulties without surrendering the ability to laugh.

"You let Felicity win? How could you let her win?" Isabel groaned as she approached after calling for an intermission at the toy theater. "Her ego is going to be unbearable for weeks."

Felicity merely shrugged and continued strutting up and down beside their card table while Clara had already floated away to seek a new form of entertainment. "I would have been just as unbearable had I lost."

"And need I remind you that none of the rest of you live with her?" Mercy added from her own card table at the other end of the room, where she played quadrille with Ellen and Isabel's aunt and younger brother.

"We shall pray ardently for you tonight," Lydia quipped.

Gentle fingers brushed against hers. Lydia started and looked up. Sebastian tugged at the cards she indignantly clutched, his eyes never leaving hers, and added them to the stack he'd already collected.

"If you would excuse me, I believe I have another engagement with two very persistent young misses," he said as he finished tidying up the cards for whoever wished to play next.

"I shall join you if you do not mind."

The words slipped from Lydia's lips unexpectedly. She opened her mouth to change her mind, yet the moment she saw Sebastian's wide, boyish smile, all of Lydia's convictions and concerns disappeared. True, she did not have much personal experience with children, and the Harrowsmiths' picnic had been one of her longest exchanges with a toddler. Surely, playing drama with dolls could not be much more difficult or embarrassing.

Besides, Lydia still hoped to be a mother herself one day…a mother not quite like her own. Perhaps now was as good a time as any to begin practicing. And who better with whom to practice than her oldest and dearest friend?

"I will never mind any time you choose to join me, Lydia."

Everything went still and quiet for a moment inside and around Lydia. The candlelight spread throughout the room concentrated into a golden glow as she stared at Sebastian, at his soft gaze and inviting smile. Had he ever said something quite so…*romantic* to her? Had he ever looked at her with so much longing?

Sebastian held out a hand, tilted his face down ever so slightly, and raised a brow. Was Lydia fabricating these signals when she had gone her whole life without putting any deeper thought into Sebastian's words and behavior? Were a few pretty words from a strange letter all it took for Lydia to upend everything she thought she had known?

"I do think an evening at the theater is just what we need, do you not agree?" he asked loudly, exaggerating a glance over his shoulder at his nieces. The girls perked up and began racing around the toy theater, cheering.

The world resumed its normal speed, bursting with lighthearted laughter and contented chatter once more. Lydia shook her head and smoothed the front of her skirts. She had never enjoyed losing herself in thought in public, even more so now that she could not be sure which emotions would be displayed on her face. Even her diligent training in ladylike expressions was apparently no match for the fog that occasionally overtook her mind or the warmth that flooded her from head to foot at the strangest moments.

"Lydia?" Sebastian whispered.

Even in the way he said her name, she could hear his concern. She could hear him asking if she was unwell, if something bothered her, if he could fetch anything for her. *No*, Lydia thought to herself, a smile tugging at the corners of her mouth. She was perfectly well, nothing bothered her, and she could not ask anything more of Sebastian than he had already given.

"Yes, I have been so longing to see the latest production by the enormously talented Miss Dorothy and Miss Christina," Lydia announced. She took Sebastian's hand, ignoring how intimate it suddenly felt to walk arm in arm with a man, their shoulders bumping and sides brushing against each other.

"Bilboquet!" the older girl cried when Sebastian and Lydia arrived. "Uncle Sebastian, can we play bilboquet?" Her younger sister had already snatched up the wooden toy, swinging the ball this way and that without any apparent attempt to land it on the stick.

"After Miss Dailey and I have gotten dressed up for the theater?" Sebastian frowned, removing an invisible top hat.

Lydia watched from the corner of her eye as he effortlessly fell into the girls' imaginary world. She continued to watch as he crossed to the far wall, opened a large, wooden chest, and returned with three more toys.

A beautifully carved handle with a smooth ball dangling by a string appeared in Lydia's hand. "O-Oh, I do not think I should—"

"First one to catch their ball wins! Go!" Miss Dorothy cheered, having already given herself a head start to master her bilboquet.

The uncertainty freezing Lydia turned to dread when she felt a particular pair of eyes boring into her from the smaller card table in the opposite corner. Lydia dared a glance out of her peripheral vision. Mother glared a snowstorm at Lydia over the top of her cards, each perfectly spaced. The sight of her respectable daughter with a toy in her hand must have been infuriatingly foreign. Of course Lydia had played with them as a child, just not where her mother could see.

Even amongst their old country friends on a relaxed evening meant to be enjoyable and lively, Lydia was always to be the exception.

"Do you require a reminder of how to play?"

Sebastian's large hand wrapped around Lydia's. Before she knew it, Lydia found herself in the very center of shrill, endearing chaos. Miss Dorothy and Miss Christina squealed with joy and skipped about her in a circle.

"Be careful with those when you are near others!" she called above the din.

A laugh boomed through the room. Every eye turned to Sebastian for a brief moment before returning to their own amusements. All except Mother's, which seemed able to simultaneously observe Lydia's every mistake without losing focus on whatever conversation or pastime engaged her. Every observation would be stored in her infallible memory to be dissected and thrown in Lydia's face later.

"Then perhaps you require a reminder of the welts we used to leave on each other when we played bilboquet?"

"Shh," Lydia hissed, trailing off in a stifled giggle. "The difference is that I have since matured."

"Miss Dailey, why aren't you playing?" Sebastian's older niece whined.

Forgetting his own bilboquet, Sebastian stepped up behind Miss Dorothy and rested his hands on her shoulders. "Yes, please play with us, Miss Dailey. *Please?*"

Lydia clenched her teeth to keep from bursting into a cloud of butterflies. How devious, joining forces against her with their beseeching pouts and entirely too adorable, round eyes! Even little Miss Christina tottered over, simply happy to participate.

"Only because you asked so politely."

Sebastian and the girls cheered and quickly returned to their toys. The bilboquet felt familiar enough in Lydia's grip as she gave the wooden ball a few hesitant swings. Her first genuine attempt, stiff-armed and head craned back nervously, resulted in the ball bouncing limply along on its string. Lydia wrinkled her nose and wondered how she had ever enjoyed this.

Sebastian chuckled. "You will have to put forth more effort than that."

Embarrassment prickled at Lydia's skin. Half-turning away to block her next sad attempt from view, she observed her friend's technique. Indeed, a light sheen of sweat had collected at his temples, tufts of black hair sticking to his skin. His every movement was somehow both easy and full of purpose. Even his feet never ceased moving as he continuously reassessed his position in relation to the elusive ball. The children did the same, running all over the rug, laughing and shrieking.

Lydia's grip tightened around the handle. She must have looked like that, been that free and passionate at some point in the past. For just tonight, with a silly, little toy in her hand and her best friend by her side, perhaps she could feel a bit like that again.

"Very close, Dorothy, very close!" Sebastian applauded his niece's effort, grinning from ear to ear.

A welcome surge of invigoration rushed through Lydia. She turned to face the others once more, Mother's judgements and anticipated scoldings to her back. Slowly engaging her entire body, Lydia soon found a flow, chest rising and falling faster, smile widening. She did not care what anyone else thought, no matter how many times she missed the ball.

No one was more surprised than Lydia herself when the ball's small opening finally caught on the tip of the handle. Mouth ajar, she stared at the bilboquet.

"I did it," she mumbled under her breath. She could hardly remember the last time she had attempted this game, let alone played it successfully. "I did it!"

Sebastian, Miss Dorothy, and Miss Christina froze, their attention snapping to Lydia. The trio swarmed her with congratulations, the younger girl throwing her arms around Lydia's legs and knocking the ball off-center once more. Her own laugh mingled with theirs, quieter yet no less cheery for once.

"What has Miss Dailey won for her brilliant success?" Sebastian asked, cheeks tinged with red, but the young ones had already started the next round.

"Your admiration is all the reward I need, dear Sebastian."

For the second time that evening, Lydia found herself biting her tongue against heedless words. Yet when Sebastian held her gaze instead of laughing the comment away or teasing her, the nerves hollowing her stomach eased away. Perhaps these were words she did not need to regret, not now.

"You have always had my admiration and you always will," he replied quietly. "Just like you will always win against me."

Sebastian's expression closed off as he reached down, his hand brushing against Lydia's dress, and returned her victorious ball to its rightful perch. Without another word, he turned back to rejoin the girls. Instead of confusion or worry, the look sparked something else inside Lydia: hope.

Hope seemed just as foolish of an emotion at this point in her life as these children's games. At least it would have before Lady Swan's letter had disrupted the melancholy contentment and grudging acceptance Lydia had developed over the Seasons. Perhaps even now it was only positioning her to fail spectacularly when she could no longer separate her own feelings from the mess she was in.

It was just a toy.

It was just a game.

It was just Sebastian.

She did not even know why hope should strike her now. Sebastian had not looked or sounded like his usual self. There had been a heaviness in his words, shadows in his eyes that would not let her see beyond. She recognized it. His eyes were mirrors of her own.

That strange, little thing, hope, whispered possibilities in the back of Lydia's mind. Normally, she cared little for being wrong.

How wonderful might it be to be wrong about this?

# CHAPTER ELEVEN

ANOTHER BALLROOM BRIMMING with Society's finest and all the food and drink anyone could dream of, and Sebastian's eyes still went straight to Lydia. She and her family stood by a sideboard on the opposite wall, conversing with the host and hostess and sipping punch. As usual, Lydia stood still and regal, the shimmering thread and jewels sewn into her ivory gown glinting under the chandelier, blinding Sebastian to all else.

He had not seen her since his family's card party for the Bainbridge friends almost a week ago. During the Season, it was not unusual for them to go that long without happening upon each other at an event or carving out some time during their hectic schedules for a chat. Never had Sebastian felt that separation more keenly.

Had something been slowly shifting between him and Lydia without him realizing? Sebastian had relived the card party and their sprightly game of bilboquet too much, blurring it all together until he had begun to wonder if he had dreamt it all up.

"Enjoy yourself, my son," Mama said, breaking Sebastian out of his daze. "And do try to dance with Miss Woods tonight. I promised her mother you would," she threw over her shoulder as she made her way to a nearby gathering of matrons cooing over the dozens of young couples spinning and sparkling.

Her suggestion made almost no impression upon Sebastian. Lydia must have noticed their arrival.

No, that day, full of Lydia's laughter, had not been a dream. What she had said…that had not been a dream, either. Smiling at Sebastian from across the ballroom, Lydia had never looked more real. Why should she seek his admiration when she herself was always the most stunning and fascinating person in any room?

Just as Sebastian took a step toward her, Lydia excused herself from her parents' conversation and took her own step. They met in the middle of a cluster of round tables.

"I am so glad you are here," Lydia started, a smile spreading across her face.

Sebastian returned it gladly. "As am I." A full smile rarely graced Lydia's lips when others beyond her Bainbridge friends were present.

A surreptitious glance to the dance floor did not escape Sebastian's notice. "Would you like to—"

"Someone has asked for my next dance," Lydia rushed in a whisper.

"Ah, wonderful." Sebastian forced the smile to remain on his face.

Whatever this new current was between them, nothing had been made clear yet. Sebastian could simply be fooling himself, caught up in Lady Swan's promises. As far as he knew, Lydia still looked at every gentleman as a potential answer to her quandary. Besides, Sebastian had had a lifetime of playing the role of supportive friend. He must still be that for Lydia, regardless of his own heart.

The lady shook her head and lowered her eyes, diamonds and sapphires twisting in the light. "I doubt that very much. Apparently, I am to dance with Viscount Cleasehill."

Something squeezed Sebastian's chest. "He has returned from the West Indies?"

"Just two days ago, it would seem. Lord and Lady Hammonton announced the surprise not long after we arrived. The ball is in his honor to welcome him home. Mother had them introduce us the moment we arrived. I was not yet out when he embarked on his journey. He is an interesting and…voluble gentleman."

Sebastian's upper lip curled as he eyed the elegant crowd for Lord Cleasehill, the future Earl of Hammonton. Lydia offered a helpful nod toward a particularly lively group of gentlemen. The tall viscount's animated gestures and raucous laughter singled him out from the men surrounding him.

Though he had never met the oldest son and heir of the evening's hosts, word of Lord Cleasehill's adventures on the other side of the world had often trickled through various gentlemen at Brooks's. Based on those few tidbits, Sebastian had contented himself with never making the viscount's acquaintance.

His focus returned to Lydia and his heart twisted. She eyed Lord Cleasehill's group, hands clasped politely before her, thumbs nervously twiddling.

"If you do not wish to dance with him, you must say so. Even your mother is sure to understand if the gentleman truly makes you uncomfortable," Sebastian insisted, fighting the urge to envelop her into arms he knew without a shadow of a doubt would protect and honor her until his last breath.

Lydia shook her head again, defeat etched on her face. "My comfort has long since fallen to the bottom of the list of requirements. In fact, I am not sure it has ever been on the list…not when Mother's need for a titled son-in-law takes up the majority. Even Father informed me earlier that Lord Cleasehill intends to travel back and forth between England and the West Indies but would not force a wife to endure such a long journey by sea. Perhaps, if I am lucky, I will only have to see him for six or so months in the year."

Sebastian scoffed, his ears ringing with the incredulity, the cruelty of it all. "That is half your life, Lydia. They cannot mean for you to be miserable for half your life."

"They would, if it would put an end to the embarrassment I bring to my family by remaining unmarried at three-and-twenty. And put an end to my mother's desperate need to boast that her grandson shall one day bear the word 'lord' before his name." She paused, looking down at the polished floor. "There is the letter to consider as well."

"No."

Lydia's head snapped up to stare at him.

"No," Sebastian continued, the heat of injustice seeping deep into his muscles. "This is not what Lady Swan wants. It cannot be. How can Lord Cleasehill be considered 'nearer than you think'? You only met the man tonight."

Somehow, despite the many times he and Lydia had had similar conversations since her first unsuccessful Season, such a terrible thought had not crossed Sebastian's mind.

He could no longer bear the pain of taking his affections for Lydia to the grave when she finally made her long-awaited match. That had always been his plan. He could not bear the mere idea of her caged in an unwanted and unhappy marriage to a man who was so blind to her wonders that he would be content to leave her behind for months on end…or worse.

Lydia gave a rueful smile. "He is nearer than he was before now that he has returned. How can you be so sure Lady Swan doesn't mean the viscount? Do you have anything you wish to confess about secret identities?"

"Refuse to dance with him." Sebastian's fists clenched at his sides.

"Then I will be required to refuse anyone else who may express interest," Lydia whispered. "You are well aware of that."

Bright-blue eyes glanced up at Sebastian. Hesitant…hopeful? Or did Sebastian only wish to transmute her pain and distress into his own selfish desires? How could he even be thinking such things now when the full extent of Mr. and Mrs. Dailey's disregard for their daughter's wellbeing had finally been revealed?

Sebastian lowered his head and fixed his gaze on his gleaming, black shoes. Of course Lydia was correct. It would be horribly offensive for a young lady to deny one gentleman, even with good reason, only to prance about the floor in the arms of another for the whole of London to see. Despite their bravado and clubs and duels, men of the *ton* could be some of the most sensitive creatures to walk the Earth.

"Only one with Lord Cleasehill tonight, I think," Lydia said softly. "If you would be so kind as to claim my next two dances?"

Sebastian's heart fluttered back to life. "Of course," he blurted out. "Anything to rescue you from that man. I only wish I could have done so sooner."

"Mother would not have allowed you." Lydia chuckled, the sound devoid of humor. "She was absolutely adamant and rather hopeful that a gentleman swiftly approaching his fortieth year must be experiencing the call of time's cruel march and will have whittled his matrimonial requirements down quite severely."

The very thought made Sebastian's throat constrict. He could hardly bring to mind another woman who would no doubt so admirably exceed any man's expectations for his wife and the mother of his children. The wild idea that he should suggest a physician's assessment for Mrs. Dailey galloped through Sebastian's mind.

How could she see only fault when Sebastian witnessed the perfection Lydia fought for every day?

"Miss Dailey?"

Ice flooded Sebastian's veins. His gaze locked with Lydia's. Together, they turned and faced Viscount Cleasehill.

Sebastian could only watch in silent dismay as another man led his dearest friend into what looked like a horrible trap.

"He has been forced upon Lydia as well, I see."

Miss Mercy Reeve appeared at Sebastian's side, a cold glower on her face. "Lady Eldmar has also forced Felicity and me to 'make any impression at all upon someone.' Clearly, she has not spent enough time in the company of my lovely twin recently. No one can walk away from her without an impression. But her dances will come later and I am praying for an unobstructed view of that indelicate Lord Cleasehill's reaction to Felicity's histrion-ics."

A muffled laugh eased some of the tension in Sebastian's

chest. "As will I," he agreed.

Relief and guilt battled for dominance in the forefront of his mind. At least Lydia was not alone in this experience. It seemed quite a few impatient mamas also found the future earl an appealing prospect for their perpetually unmarried daughters now that he had returned from the West Indies with even grander wealth to add to his family's name.

Yet the idea of any other lady being left to that fate unwillingly left a bitter taste in Sebastian's mouth. There must have been some young fortune-huntress in Society who would be thrilled to remove Lord Cleasehill from the marriage mart in exchange for a lifetime of luxury as the future Countess of Hammonton.

"Dear Mr. Harrowsmith, would you be willing to have a word with our Isabel?" Miss Mercy continued, a hint of concern beneath the surface of her words. "She has always favored practical considerations, especially after… If you are in possession of any information that might overrule such considerations in regards to Lord Cleasehill…."

"You have my word," Sebastian hurried to say. Without properly excusing himself, he wove through the crowd in the direction Miss Mercy had nodded.

"Miss Abbott, there you are," Sebastian called when he spied the lady pressed against the wall in the corner taking measured sips of her drink. "Please tell me you are not dancing with Lord Cleasehill," he added under his breath as soon as he came within earshot.

The lady's brows arched. She led them farther into the corner beside a small, round table bearing a mound of untouched cucumber sandwiches. "Not until later in the evening," she answered, glancing down at her dance card.

"Allow me to dissuade you from any attraction you may feel on the basis of his material qualities," he continued in a rush, choosing his words with care. "I have heard far too much about that gentleman from others in my circle to encourage any friend of mine in his direction. Excessive drinking, boorish treatment of his social inferiors, incivility toward his few social superiors, taking greater liberties with the ladies there than he would ever dare here… I am sure you will understand if I withhold the details."

"Thank you, Mr. Harrowsmith," Miss Abbott exhaled, eyes wide. "I may have slightly different interests in a husband than our other friends, but my practicality extends beyond the physical and social comforts. Even if Lord Cleasehill could exceed all my earthly needs and desires at a moment's notice, I could never hold myself with pride again were I to become his wife."

"I am immensely happy to be of service," Sebastian said with a nod. At the very least, he could act as Lady Swan's opposite for the Bainbridge girls, steering them away from unsuitable gentlemen.

Sebastian's ears perked the moment the music had ceased. Again without excusing himself properly, he rushed toward the center of the ballroom, weaving through huddles of conversing guests in their dazzling finery, completely unconcerned with the panic that propelled him. He knew his friends would not fault him for his abrupt departures.

Squeezing between a trio of wobbly, older gentlemen and a clearly enamored courting couple taking advantage of the crowd to covertly hold hands, Sebastian slammed into the wall of a menacing presence. He came to a dead halt. Mrs. Dailey had won the race.

No spine had ever looked more excruciatingly rigid as she waited at the edge of the dance floor to ensnare Lydia yet again. Sebastian could easily imagine the preternatural vexation that was as much a feature of Mrs. Dailey's countenance as her nose.

His heart tumbled to the floor. Why did he always feel as if he were just on the other side, as if he had just missed it by a moment?

They both watched, Sebastian in her shadow. Lydia offered a curtsey to Lord Cleasehill, her expression graceful despite the strain that was evident to Sebastian alone. Lord Cleasehill merely smirked in response and swished a hand through the air as he unceremoniously left Lydia on the dance floor.

Anger surged up from somewhere deep in Sebastian's chest. How unspeakably rude! To not even escort one's partner off the dance floor, no matter how unbearable the partner or dance had been? For a true gentleman, such a thing would have been inconceivable.

The lady stood frozen while the other dancers filtered around her with pitying frowns. Sebastian had never seen such a crestfallen, embarrassed expression on that face he longed to stare at for the rest of time. He never wanted to see that look again. He must do everything in his power to prevent it.

"Lydia," Mrs. Dailey called quietly, slicing through the noise.

Lowering her head, Lydia obeyed, lifeless. Sebastian doubted he could feel any lower than he did now.

The older woman whispered something in her daughter's ear, sharp and threatening. Even from here, Sebastian could see the force it took for Lydia to raise her head once more. In just that moment, her expression had turned neutral, as if she could not feel the prying eyes in every direction.

Still Sebastian could see—no, *sense*—the sheer tension preventing Lydia from falling apart into mortification. He could read her very thoughts, feel the shame of having such a distasteful man discard her so openly, at the very center of a ballroom brimming with the *ton*.

To his horror, Lydia turned in the direction Lord Cleasehill had gone, squeezing her eyes shut before fixing them upon the viscount once more. She walked slowly as Mrs. Dailey watched, the ice in her glare masked by marble elegance—to all except Sebastian.

He could abide it no longer. Someone must finally say something to the woman. How could she think of sending Lydia straight back to the man who had just authored her greatest humiliation?

Lydia would always obey, no matter the cost. She had long

since stopped wishing for her mother's innate approval and had accepted the burden of earning it instead. Somehow, it was the one thing she and Sebastian had never openly discussed. Even between them, some things were too painful for words. He knew without knowing how it was the only other thing Lydia truly wanted after finding a love match. To achieve both in one fell swoop was no doubt her dearest dream of all.

Sebastian only managed a few firm steps toward Mrs. Dailey when a pompous, nasally voice stopped both him and Lydia in their tracks.

"Her? Good heavens, *her?* No, no, I think not." Lord Cleasehill snorted, his back to Sebastian, Lydia, and her mother. He flapped a hand when one of his companions spotted their small audience, unconcerned.

"When we arrived at the subject of art, she informed me that her favorite painter is that strange Mr. Euston fellow. A few gentlemen I know in the West Indies have hung his paintings in their homes. They say Euston's work reminds them fondly of England—cold and dreadfully dull. Just like Miss Dailey." Smirking, the future earl ran a hand through gray-tinged hair and plucked a drink from a passing footman's tray.

The immediate area fell into a shocked hush. Sebastian looked to Lydia, a vise of panic crushing his entire body. All the color had drained from Lydia's face. She stared at Lord Cleasehill with wide eyes.

Finally, one of the other men's frantic gesturing and the stillness in their vicinity convinced Lord Cleasehill to turn around. He jutted his chin in the air and gazed back at Lydia down a long, narrow nose.

"I am afraid I do not have any other dances to spare tonight. Seek charity elsewhere, hmm?"

Sebastian's stomach burst into flames as it turned itself inside out over and over again. Shadows filled the corners of his vision, capturing that revolting man in his sights and banishing all else. "How dare—"

"You should apologize to me at once, my lord."

Ripples of whispers dispelled the shocked silence. Sebastian could feel the weight of the entire room's attention at his back, barreling toward Lydia.

When he looked at her again, Sebastian found her standing exactly where she was. Yet her whole demeanor had transformed. She returned Lord Cleasehill's derision with cool dignity. Her eyes darted to Sebastian. For once, he could not interpret their meaning.

"I beg your pardon?" The viscount forced a laugh, the muscles in his fleshy face twitching.

"You should apologize to me, but I know you will not. Instead, I shall only say that it is a shame these are the manners you choose to display to the people of the West Indies, to the people of the world which you are privileged to experience. To the very people here tonight who have awaited your return and welcomed you home. I shall sleep none the worse tonight for your judgements, knowing that I showed you nothing but courtesy—a concept with which you might consider reacquainting yourself."

Gasps resounded across the room, including Mrs. Dailey's. All the while, Lydia forced Lord Cleasehill to look her in the eyes, holding her head high. All the while, with every eloquent word that spilled forth, a glow enveloped her, growing in strength and spirit.

Sebastian's heart grew with it, a familiar warmth washing away the raging heat of anger. A smile tugged at the corner of his mouth. *What a fascinating prospect*, he thought to himself, *that one could spend a lifetime beside another and still stumble upon breathtaking surprises.*

He had been entirely truthful with Lydia at the card party. He had always admired her deep in his bones. Now his admiration went deeper still, seeping into a foundation of which he had not fully realized the vastness until this moment.

"Heavens above," came an astonished whisper from Sebastian's left. Miss Felicity Reeve stared open-mouthed, completely still. Miss Mercy mirrored her expression. Once Lydia discovered she held such power over the most unruly member of their group, Miss Reeve's boasts of whist victories could hardly hope to compete.

The other girls had joined from various corners of the ballroom. Poor Miss Gardiner had a hand clasped over her mouth, tears at the corners of her eyes. Her younger sister had one arm wrapped around her waist while Miss Abbott grasped her other hand tightly.

"I beg your forgiveness, my lord, truly." Mrs. Dailey jerked forward, still recovering from her own shock. "My daughter is overtired, that is all."

"If you will please excuse me," Lydia announced as she curtseyed, true to her impeccable propriety even now. She spun on her heel, silk skirts swishing, and marched past her mother toward the ballroom doors. The crush of guests parted for her, every expression perplexed rather than offended. Some even watched her stride past with astonished respect.

The moment she was out of view, Sebastian rounded on Lord Cleasehill. He kept the viscount in his sights as air slowly filled the room once more. The musicians hesitantly resumed at Lady Hammonton's frantic urging. Dodging dazed guests gossiping behind their hands, Sebastian followed that dreadful man as he stomped through the ballroom toward the double doors. The gathering afforded Lord Cleasehill a wide berth, not quite looking him in the eye.

"How dare you speak to her like that?" Sebastian growled through gritted teeth the moment the double doors closed behind him, sealing them in the shadows of the empty hallway. His teeth ground into each other even harder to fight a laugh as the older man sputtered, hastily dabbing at dribbles of the brandy he had been sipping.

"I am afraid, my lord, that you have grown accustomed to keeping company you consider beneath you as the heir to an earldom, strutting about a foreign land. You seem to think the principles of civility and kindness need not cross the ocean with you simply because there is almost no one on the other side wealthy and well-connected enough to challenge you," Sebastian spat under his breath. His chest rose and fell faster, every inch of his being tense.

"Let this serve as a reminder, Lord Cleasehill, that you are in England now—in the very heart of the *ton*, as a matter of fact." He raised an arm toward the ballroom behind them, already alive with the sounds of merrymaking once more. "Perhaps I am the only one who is not enamored with your outlandish stories and successes and therefore am the only one who will not tolerate such abhorrent slander. You could never hope to be deserving of Miss Dailey, and her life shall be all the happier for your absence. I strongly urge you to use the influence to which you cling to publicly accept the blame for this display as yours alone and absolve Miss Dailey of any wrongdoing."

The longer Sebastian spoke, the lower the viscount's mouth dropped open. His eyes bulged, sweat-tinged skin growing redder under the flicker of a distant sconce. "H-How dare *you* speak to *me* like that?!"

"It was not difficult in the least. Not where Miss Dailey is concerned."

Lord Cleasehill's weather-worn features crunched into a scowl. "If you think so highly of her, why did you leave her in my way to waste my time?" he snapped. "Or are you the type of bachelor who is protective of his array of options?"

Sebastian felt no sting from the underhanded insult. He only felt the resounding fact of his answer.

There were no options but Lydia. She would always be his only one.

"If I apologize for bruising your ego, will you finally allow me to pass?" Lord Cleasehill grumbled.

"A man's emotions hold no importance when a lady has been treated so hideously before such an audience. Any lady."

The man snarled and shoved past Sebastian toward the ballroom doors. Nearly half his drink splashed across Sebastian's shoulder and chest, sticky against his hot skin. Grimacing, Sebastian took a stumbling half-step back and bumped into something soft.

"Sebastian…."

Lydia emerged from the shadows, brows upturned and lips parted. The pearls in her hair glowed soft yellow. Her cheeks looked warm to the touch.

"You should not have heard all that, Lydia," Sebastian mumbled, pain lancing him. "You should never have to hear such things."

Once again, he forced his eyes to his shoes. Holding her gaze was both too exhilarating and too excruciating.

"Sebastian, I do not know what to say," she whispered.

"Forgive me for speaking so impertinently—"

A dainty hand darted out and captured Sebastian's fingers, slowly intertwining hers with his. Lydia held on tightly, giving an encouraging squeeze when her immobile friend refused to look up.

Sebastian forced his eyes to meet hers. To finally see it—the hope of love reflected back to him.

Something wild seized him. Heart hammering at a thrilling speed, he cupped Lydia's face in both hands. Their gazes did not break. Despite the impulse tingling under the surface of his skin, Sebastian was not surprised. Nor was Lydia. Peace settled over her delicate features, soft in the low light. She felt so perfect against him like this.

She felt even more perfect, unimaginably perfect, when she finally pressed her lips to his.

They moved together slowly, in no rush after a lifetime of waiting for this moment. Without a word needing to pass between them, a sublime contentment enveloped them both, the feeling of all Sebastian's dreams coming true.

Alongside them, promises bloomed—promises of the future he had only dared visit on the nights when sleep had eluded him.

They never failed to lull him into a hazy rendition of this present reality. There was no haze now, only the most profound clarity Sebastian had ever encapsulated in words, a clarity he poured into this kiss with the force of every lost dream bursting back into life.

When they pulled apart, Lydia's cheeks flushed. Sebastian savored the anticipation for a breath longer as he stared at this incredible, beautiful woman. In another moment, the change they had begun would be made official, permanent.

"Lydia, I—"

"There you are, you ungrateful creature!"

Sebastian and Lydia jolted, foreheads colliding. Panic won out over the pain as Sebastian took a wide step to the side, hoping the shadows would create the illusion of distance. An empty hallway outside a ballroom was no place to announce a new courtship, especially not after all that unpleasant business.

Mrs. Dailey stormed at them, a vein pulsing in the center of her forehead that Sebastian had never seen before and hoped never to see again. She was terrifying. "Home. Now."

Lydia bowed her head and glanced at Sebastian. He read the caution there. Anything either of them said now would only serve to infuriate Mrs. Dailey further. He pursed his lips together as Lydia retreated down the hall behind her mother, biting back the vitriol he longed to fling at the woman as she berated Lydia for leaving her to beg their hosts' forgiveness alone.

They had not yet had an opportunity to arrange further plans. Sebastian had not a clue when he would see Lydia again. The prospect was torturous in a strangely thrilling way.

At least now he knew no partings with the one who held his heart, a heart he hoped he could finally bring into the light very soon, would be permanent. Not once Sebastian finally finished telling Lydia what had been waiting on the tip of his tongue since he could speak.

# Chapter Twelve

LYDIA'S HEART DANCED, her stomach wound unbearably tight, as the driver helped her down from the carriage outside the Reeve family's townhouse. For once, it was not an unpleasant sensation. Not entirely, at least.

She had had to work quickly and craftily, deploying the most trusted staff in her household to fly to her friends' homes in the early hours of the morning, while the rest of the *ton*—and most importantly, their parents—slept soundly. Still, Lydia knew she could only count on the discretion of footmen and maids so much. Eventually, Mother would catch wind of Lydia's early adventure.

After Lydia's shameful outburst at Lord and Lady Hammonton's ball the night before, her mother had locked Father and Edmund out of her sitting room to give Lydia a tongue-lashing like she had never received before. In fact, Mother had yelled and criticized for so long—including entirely plausible threats to keep Lydia within sight at all times for the rest of her life, whether she married or not—that the sun had just barely begun to tinge the London fog in silver by the time she had worn herself down. That left Lydia with just enough time to frantically write her letters. She gave the footmen a signal the moment Mother had retreated to her quarters to finally sleep.

Felicity and Mercy's home, being most central to them all, had long since become their meeting place or point of origin for other activities. As she followed the seemingly unfazed butler to Lord and Lady Eldmar's drawing room, Lydia prayed the others had already arrived. Time was not her companion today.

"Here she is!"

"Shh!" Mercy hissed at her sister, forcibly lowering Felicity's arm that had stretched toward the door, pointing at Lydia accusingly. "Do you wish to awaken the entire house?"

"Lydia, what on Earth is this all about?" Ellen asked, eyes wide with worry as she snatched a candle away from the dangling sleeve of Felicity's robe.

Lydia held up her hands for silence. She suddenly needed to catch her breath, to steady her spinning mind. Her complete lack of sleep was only one small factor.

Most of it, of course, was all Sebastian's fault. And she could not have been more grateful.

A smile cracked on her lips. It spread across her face, from cheek to cheek, a truly unladylike grin.

Isabel gasped, inching to the very edge of her chair, a hand over her mouth. "Lydia...something has happened. What has happened?" she cried in a quiet whisper.

The other girls all watched her with bated breath, Felicity and Mercy squeezing hands, Ellen fanning herself, and Clara biting down hard on her bottom lip. They looked as though they expected Lydia to announce that by some strange legal mishap, she suddenly found herself in line to be the next Queen of England.

Laughter bubbled from somewhere deep in her chest. Only someone who had gone well and truly mad would find that scenario of secondary preference to the incredible reality that had swept her off her feet the night before. *No*, Lydia thought as she let the sound spill into the anticipating silence of the drawing room. *Why would I want the Crown Jewels when I have the brightest jewel of all: Sebastian's heart?*

"Someone has asked to court you," Clara squeaked, both fists clenched before her mouth. "That must be it. Is it?"

As much as Lydia surprisingly found herself enjoying the suspense she had built, she knew the feeling of a secret shared and met with joy and love must be even better. Besides, poor Clara looked fit to burst with excitement at any moment.

"Better than that," Lydia teased, unable to help it. Just a second more could not hurt.

Her friends leaned forward in their seats, eyes wide and mouths agape. A blurry memory of them all seated together on the floor of a nursery room, she could not recall which, enraptured by the governess's story of a princess falling in love with her gallant knight, flashed through Lydia's mind. Now it was her turn to stun them with a story of fantastical romance. At least it still felt like a fantasy to Lydia despite the hundreds of times she must have replayed it in her mind to drown out Mother's berating.

"Sebastian kissed me."

Cheers and squeals of delight erupted throughout the drawing room. Clara shot to her feet. "He *kissed* you?! Oh, Lydia, what a joyous day! When will you marry?"

Lydia let her head fall back as her friends squeezed another laugh out of her, all of them wrapping their arms around her in a lovingly suffocating embrace. Abuzz with glee and unable to contain it any longer, Clara began bouncing on her toes. Everyone else joined in, jostling Lydia in the middle, giggling and accidentally stepping on each other's toes.

When was the last time they had all done something so frivolous and free? When was the last time Lydia had enjoyed anything without a single worry? Was this what living a life free to be herself, as Sebastian had always said she ought to, could be like?

"We are not marrying," Lydia managed to gasp out. Her friends released her and gaped. "At least, I do not know when yet," she hurried to add. "He did not propose, you see."

As the news settled, the ladies resumed their seats. Lydia took a chair toward the center, all eyes on her. "I feel positive he would have if Mother had not come storming out of the ballroom," she grumbled.

"I must confess I feared the worst for you," said Mercy, fiddling with the frills of her sleeves. "But perhaps I should not have after seeing the way you rose to your own defense against that dreadful Lord Cleasehill."

"So brave!" Clara agreed, cheeks flushed.

"Admirable indeed, Lydia." Felicity nodded, the fire bright in her eyes despite the unnaturally early hour. "I only wish I had such an opportunity to share my mind! And he had the audacity to sulk about the ballroom for the remainder of the evening, bemoaning his injured feelings to anyone witless enough to come near."

Lydia held up her hands, a warm mixture of pride and embarrassment spreading through her. "Thank you, ladies, but I can hardly fathom what came over me and I do not believe my actions are worthy of praise. The only good to come of it all was Sebastian's kiss."

"What was that like?" Ellen asked breathlessly.

"How did it all come about?" Isabel raised her voice. "Answer that first, and then...." She trailed off, shrugging in Ellen's direction with an apologetic smile. Lydia had long since suspected that out of all of them—until today—Isabel was the only one of them who could have answered Ellen's question. She was the only one who had been courted before. But Isabel had never spoken of those days in detail and none of them would have dreamed of exploiting her pain for their curiosity.

Lydia explained it all, starting from her dramatic exit from the ballroom, which they had all witnessed. The girls hung on every word and Ellen looked on the verge of swooning herself.

"And then Mother spotted us and dragged me home," Lydia finished in a rush. The story had fallen from her lips in one long breath.

"Did she not see you together?" Mercy asked, brows raised incredulously.

Lydia shook her head quickly, shuddering at the thought.

"Heavens, no. Nor does it seem as though she suspects anything. She must have assumed Sebastian was comforting me, which is essentially true. Naturally, she is far more enraged by my behavior toward the future Earl of Hammonton in his own home in front of half the *ton*'s eligible gentlemen than the fact that anyone might have happened upon Sebastian and me in the shadows. She sometimes forgets that not everyone in Society knows that we are…*were* childhood friends and nothing more."

"Thank goodness for that, then." Felicity chuckled. "Otherwise, my theory as to the reason behind the sudden and secret meeting might have proven true."

"Dare I ask what that theory is?" Lydia sighed, though she did not fight the now-permanent smile on her face. She had Sebastian to thank for that.

Felicity crossed her arms over her chest and leaned back in her chair. A lock of hair curled around a rag slipped out from beneath her sleeping cap. "I suggested that you were escaping London—perhaps England altogether—before Mrs. Dailey turned you out to make a living as a governess. I swear I have never seen that perpetually vexed woman so livid and so…bright red."

"That is indeed what this meeting would have been about had she caught us." Ice shot down Lydia's back. In her mother's eyes, her tryst with Sebastian would have been the only thing worse she could have done than insulting Lord Cleasehill. Not only had Lydia dared to kiss a man in public, she had dared to kiss a man without a title.

"Enough of all that," Clara whined. She twisted a kerchief in her hands. "Tell us, Lydia…. What was the kiss like?"

A hush swept over the room. The ladies leaned forward once more, eyes alight. Lydia closed hers and inhaled, letting the memories still alive in her skin, in the tingle of her lips, flood her senses.

It only took an instant. Sebastian was never far from her mind now. In truth, Lydia had realized at some point during the long night that she had never truly stopped thinking about Sebastian since the moment she had become aware of his presence beside her. Every other thought had merely been a distraction from him.

"It was…perfect."

"Yes, but what does that *mean*?" Ellen prodded.

Lydia chuckled to herself. She could feel it all right there in her heart. She could feel everything it meant to her. Everything it meant to him. How could a handful of words encapsulate the entirety of such a feeling? Lydia had searched in English, French, and Italian. Though each language offered its own beautiful interpretations, they were just that—approximations that paled in comparison to the truth.

"Imagine something that is both so thrilling that you think it will drive you mad and so comforting that you could fall asleep in it every single night," she started quietly.

"Like…the new flavor of ice at Gunter's that everyone praises to the skies, that you are convinced cannot possibly be the wonder that they make it seem. Yet when you finally try it for yourself, in that very instant, you are forever changed. Never will another flavor of ice bring you the bliss that this one does. And you are too enchanted to bother feeling foolish for thinking everyone else was wrong."

The silence stretched on, each lady absorbing Lydia's words. Lydia did the same.

Where they had sprung from, she could not imagine. While others frequented Gunter's once a week during the Season, Lydia had only been able to sneak a bite from Sebastian's dish on the few occasions she'd accompanied his family to Society's favorite tea and dessert shop.

"Kissing sounds heavenly." Clara sighed, her brown eyes distant and tranquil.

"It is, and I pray that you all will experience it one day as well if it means for you what it means for me." Lydia offered a smile to the girls, a sudden lump of emotion lodging in her throat. "My friends, I am in love with Sebastian."

"Ahh," they sighed sweetly, the romantic Gardiner sisters

both dabbing at the corners of their eyes with kerchiefs.

"We are so, so happy for you, dearest Lydia." Mercy grinned and reached across the small table between them to squeeze Lydia's hand.

Isabel scooted closer on the sofa to Lydia's right. "And of course Mr. Harrowsmith is completely and utterly in love with you. Perhaps I can now confess that the five of us often teasingly wondered when the two of you would finally realize it."

"Was it truly so obvious?" Lydia's face flushed as she lowered her head sheepishly.

"It was obvious that he has always been a little more yours than ours," Ellen said quietly. She leaned forward and touched a gentle finger under Lydia's chin, lifting her face once more. "And that is nothing to feel foolish for, either. Everything happens in its time."

Sniffling, Lydia took Ellen's hand and pressed it to her cheek. "Thank you, darling." Ellen spoke the least of them all and always ensured that every word was worth saying.

"Surely, he will be proposing any day now," Felicity announced. "Most likely, the very next time you meet."

The older Reeve twin jumped up from her chair and began acting out Sebastian's role. With a giddy yelp, Clara joined her, taking Lydia's part with fluttering lashes and arm draped dramatically across her forehead.

"Dear Lydia, I have loved you since the moment I laid eyes on you—though you did not have any hair and never ceased crying," Felicity said, pitching her voice comically low, one arm outstretched and palm up like a stage actor.

"Oh, Sebastian!" Clara sighed, buckling at the knees.

Felicity lunged forward to catch her, both toppling to the ground in an admirable show of commitment to the drama. Laughter echoed through the drawing room, Lydia's loudest of all.

Lydia laughed so loud and for so long, she realized that she had completely forgotten what it was like to release the sensation with reckless abandon. Until a snort cut through the jubilant noise. Lydia's cheeks flamed. She laughed like this so seldomly that she had also forgotten what happened when she found something *too* amusing. Edmund had once made the mistake of referring to her little piggy laugh in Mother's presence.

"Was that our prim and proper Lydia?" Felicity gasped, her character abandoned.

Isabel giggled behind a hand. "My grandpapa did that once after drinking too much brandy."

Lydia groaned. "Please, you must never tell Sebastian."

Yes, he was her best friend. He had seen the trial and error it had taken her and her mother to mold a perfect young lady. He had watched as her flaws had been polished away—and he knew that many still existed under the smooth surface.

All that, and he still loved her. He must, though he had not had the chance to say it. A snorting laugh surely would put a damper on anyone's enthusiasm for the object of their affection, even someone as unendingly loyal as Sebastian had proven himself to be.

"Really, Lydia, did you truly think we would?" Mercy laughed.

"And if we did, do you think your Sebastian would mind?" Clara added, her face flushed with exhilaration.

*Her* Sebastian. It felt so right to call him her own and allow herself to truly be someone else's. There was safety in the vulnerable giving of oneself to someone as trusted as Sebastian. *Her* Sebastian.

"You know, I just realized something," Isabel started. She eyed Lydia with a curious frown. "Does this mean Lady Swan was correct after all?"

Lady Swan! Lydia stared back at Isabel dumbfounded. She had been so absorbed in the kiss and all she still longed to say to and do with Sebastian that the mystery letter had completely slipped her mind.

"Felicity, Mercy."

All six ladies whipped around in their seats. Lady Eldmar stood in the drawing room doorway, sleeping cap askew and silk robe pulled tight about her.

"I thought I heard a commotion and one of the footmen said you had both disappeared in here. What is the meaning of this?" With all the elegance of a heavy-eyed viscountess, she waved a hand at the gathering.

"Forgive me, my lady." Lydia rose to her feet and curtseyed to the older woman. "It was I who called us all to meet here. I am sure you recall my outburst at the ball last night. You see, I was so distraught by it all that I could hardly sleep. The company of my friends was the only thing to console me."

Lady Eldmar's gaze traveled from girl to girl, barely glancing over her own daughters, before finally returning to Lydia. "Very well. You had best return home, all of you. And pray that it seems nothing more than an odd little dream when I wake."

The viscountess spun around, robe swishing out behind her, and left the ladies alone once more. They knew better than to test Lady Eldmar and offered hurried hugs and farewells and promises to meet again as soon as possible with more exciting news.

Within the dark privacy of her family's carriage, Lydia's mind turned away from the consequences of Lady Eldmar's discovery. Everything else eased into the background as thoughts of Sebastian's welcoming, brown eyes and lively laugh and soft, sweet lips rushed forward. Her anxious heartbeat slowed to that familiar, comfortable pace she had come to associate with her dearest friend.

If this had been Lady Swan's intention all along, she had done a superb job. Lydia smiled at that bit of the letter that she returned to most often.

*"Perhaps the one you seek is nearer than you think."*

That could only mean Sebastian. It had always been Sebastian. The obvious answer had, indeed, been the correct one. Lydia's heart had known it the entire time, deep down. The spark of hope at its center had awoken the morning Lady Swan's letter had arrived.

If only she could tell him all these remarkable things this very moment! If only they could say the words they had been longing to say, knowingly and unknowingly, and begin building an intertwined future atop the foundation of their shared past.

Instead, the carriage lumbered through the dark streets of London, carrying her home to more scoldings from Mother, who could easily decide that all Lydia's friends—Sebastian included—proved too distracting for Lydia at the height of the Season and forbid her from seeing them.

Lydia straightened her back against the velvet cushions. Whatever punishment Mother had in store for her, Lydia would simply have to wait until it had run its course.

This would not stand in their way. After all, they had just overcome the most challenging obstacle of all. Perhaps if Lydia had never received Lady Swan's letter, she would have missed the very thing she had needed all along.

Now that they knew their own feelings and each other's, what could hope to keep them apart?

# Chapter Thirteen

Sebastian glanced down at his pocket watch and slowed his steps. He still had more than enough time to reach Brooks's. Besides, most of his wider friend group seemed to forget that they, too, had pocket watches chained to their vests.

Of course Sebastian had been checking his with alarming frequency of late. He watched the hands tick by, counting down the hours, and now days, since he had last seen Lydia—since he had last *kissed* Lydia.

Butterflies erupted in his stomach, his steps bouncing against the pavement. Whenever Sebastian's heart ached with the uncertainty of when he would see her again, the memories burst into color and sensation behind his eyes, no matter where he was. It was a consolation prize to ease the lifelong burning that had grown tenfold since their kiss. Somehow, knowing that she felt as he did had made distance of any time and length a Herculean trial.

Sebastian slipped the watch back into its pocket and forced his attention back to the street of shops full of strolling couples and happy families. No matter how tempting his daydreams were, he must focus if he had any hope of reaching his destination—unless he wanted to repeat yesterday's debacle of accidentally appearing at the entirely wrong townhouse on the next street over from a friend's, much to the indignation of the elderly widow and her fluffy dog within.

All because he had kissed Lydia, and she had returned the kiss with the love Sebastian had so desperately wanted to feel. Lydia occupied so much of his mind that he hardly knew where he was going anymore.

A well-known sign hanging above a shop a few doors down swung in the wind. Lydia's favorite modiste. Most gentlemen knew nothing of modistes and did not care to. But Sebastian knew that Madame Roche was Lydia's favorite—Mrs. Dailey's as well. As a result, Lydia's mother rarely found fault in her dress, a blessed relief from all the other fussing.

When he came to the window, Sebastian glanced in from the corner of his eye. His heart stuttered as a familiar outline blurred past on the other side of the glass. Half-turning, Sebastian's shoulder clipped a gentleman walking in the opposite direction.

"A thousand apologies. I seem to have lost my wits," he sputtered, bowing low. The other man grumbled something about arrogant young fops and hurried off, brushing imaginary dust from his shoulder.

Sebastian had lost his wits indeed. They had always been compromised where Lydia was concerned. He was certain his hopeless wits had floated into the sky along with his heart the moment his lips had found Lydia's.

And now he thought he saw her around every corner, in every shop window. No, of course it could not be Lydia. That would be too strange. Sebastian straightened his vest and tugged on his coat sleeves. The temptation kept him rooted to the pavement.

Just a check to confirm. Surely, that would not count against his lovestruck sanity. Sebastian's eyes darted up. Lydia's stared back through the glass.

Mouth falling open, Sebastian yanked the modiste's door open. Lydia rushed to meet him, a finger pressed to her lips. Her other hand shot out and grasped his wrist, eyes narrowing when Sebastian wiggled to loosen her grip. He seized the first opportunity to slide her hand down from his wrist and into his, wrapping his fingers securely around hers. A shy smile tugging on her lips, Lydia led Sebastian toward a back corner, away from the window and partially obscured from the rest of the shop by a large display of ribbons, lace, and silk flowers. He could just see Mrs. Dailey in the back of the shop speaking with Madame Roche herself.

"Why are you here?" Lydia whispered. The urgency in her voice did not stop her from weaving her fingers through Sebastian's.

"I could ask the same of you," Sebastian mumbled through a dazed chuckle. She looked even more beautiful than she had at the ball. Her desire for him shone clear and bright in her summer-sky, blue eyes.

Lydia tilted her head to one side, a curl slipping loose. For once, Sebastian did not fight the impulse. He reached up and brushed her cheek with a knuckle, tucking the soft strand back into the protection of her bonnet. Lydia's eyes slipped closed as she leaned into his touch.

"It is perfectly normal for a young lady to visit a modiste," she whispered, a trace of laughter in her voice.

"And it is perfectly normal for me to trail after you like a puppy."

Lydia sighed. "I missed you."

"I missed you as well. When can we speak properly? I think—at least, I hope—that we have much to discuss?"

The lady nodded, gaze soft. "We do. But I am afraid Mother has taken tighter hold of my schedule after what I said to Lord Cleasehill and then subsequently sneaking away in the early morning to meet our Bainbridge friends."

Sebastian frowned. "*What* did you do?"

Lydia's eyes darted to the floor, a pretty pink dusting her cheeks. "I had to tell them, of course. I was too excited to wait, so the moment Mother had finished lamenting my birth, sometime around sunrise, I wrote them to meet me at the Reeves' home."

"I suspect they were not surprised." Sebastian grinned, his

heart flipping. They most likely had begun suspecting his feelings years ago.

"Not in the least." Lydia returned his smile, eyes brimming with delight. "But…." She paused and glanced over Sebastian's shoulder. Mrs. Dailey leafed through a book of the Season's popular styles as the modiste explained the unique beauties of each one. "Mother has decided to take my future firmly in her own hands now. She said that if I cannot be trusted to make the correct impression on gentlemen like Lord Cleasehill, she shall do it for me. Apparently, that also means I am only to see my friends at events."

"Is she…choosing suitors for you?" Sebastian asked through gritted teeth. The flip in his heart reversed and tumbled back down to reality.

"Most likely, yes." Lydia looked down again, chewing on the inside of her bottom lip, an old habit.

Sebastian took her hands, always clad in gloves when out and about, much to his displeasure. Her head shot up, anxiety and desire battling in her gaze.

"We will find a way, a time when we can discuss two decades of things unsaid," she promised. The earnest light in her face nudged Sebastian's apprehensive heart. It stuttered into an erratic beat. He had prayed that their path would be smooth once they determined how best to approach the problem of Mrs. Dailey. But if they faced another hurdle on the way to happiness, it would be nothing compared to years of misunderstanding each other's feelings.

"Of course, dearest Lydia," Sebastian agreed, instilling every word with earnestness. He squeezed her hands a little tighter. "I do not wish to exacerbate the discord between you and your mother. Just know that my heart will ache with your absence with every breath and I shall come the moment you merely think of summoning me."

Lydia giggled, ducking her face into her shoulder to shield herself, her hands still occupied by Sebastian's. That was for the best. He always wanted to see her endearing, sweet smile and hear her perfect laugh to the fullest extent possible and always would. He wished someone in Society would deem it improper for ladies to dim their happiness behind polite hands if it meant Lydia would never have to hide her spirit ever again.

A shimmer of smooth, luxurious fabric caught the corner of Sebastian's eye. He glanced at the wall of fabrics behind Lydia, each rolled in bolts with the loose end artfully draped for customers' examination. The same silvery gleam guided his gaze down by Lydia's elbow.

The fine, blue, silk net, so pale and light, it appeared silver at a glance, contrasted beautifully with the lady's warm skin. Blue had always been his favorite color on Lydia. Every shade enhanced a different dimension in her complementary irises.

"I will wait for you, no matter how long it takes," he said under his breath. "I have had much practice." Surely, she was close enough to hear, her forehead just under the tip of his nose.

When and how had they gotten so close? Sebastian had asked himself that question over the years. Even as friends, nothing about their personalities indicated any potential for harmony. Yet they had grown side by side into the people they were now. They had witnessed every failure and triumph and crushing loss in each other's lives. They had withstood it all, withstood the test of time until they had both known it was right.

Sebastian could not begin to guess how he knew that it had been right to kiss her in the hallway outside a ballroom. It had been the same as the way he had always known somewhere deep inside that he and Lydia were, despite their differences, perfect for each other. He just knew, as if the truth had been there the entire time.

"I am so very, very glad you waited."

Soft lips brushed Sebastian's cheek, then pressed in for a blissful moment before pulling away. The spot prickled, clinging to the sensation of Lydia's kiss. Sebastian's heart jolted into a dizzying gymnastics performance the likes of which Astley's

Amphitheatre with all its wonders had never seen.

Lydia wore a shy smile. "You have absolutely made each and every one of my senses abandon me, Sebastian Harrowsmith. You have turned me as silly as you are."

Sebastian angled his face down, bringing them forehead to forehead. "You seem to be enjoying it as much as I am."

"Lydia? Where are you? Come, I have selected options for you to consider from Madame Roche's latest," Mrs. Dailey called, her voice echoing as if from a great distance.

"I hope to see you again soon," Lydia whispered, her eyes locked on Sebastian for a long moment, as if committing his features to memory.

"You will, I promise." Sebastian nodded as she lifted the hem of her skirts and turned toward the other end of the shop.

"Mr. Harrowsmith. How interesting coming across you here," Mrs. Dailey mused when she spotted him approaching behind Lydia.

Sebastian's spine straightened under her hard, scrutinizing glare. "Indeed. I happened to be on my way to Brooks's when I spied you both here. At that precise moment, I remembered that my younger niece has been taken with lace recently, so I thought I would see if Miss Dailey had any suggestions that might please the dear little thing without falling to pieces in a few days."

The lie slipped out of Sebastian easily. It was necessary, he reminded himself, to keep Mrs. Dailey out of their affairs. The moment she caught any indication of interest in either direction, she would charge full steam ahead at the altar, dragging her daughter to the feet of the first lord who would have her. She would be another's wife before they had an opportunity to proclaim their love for the first time.

They did love each other, and in the end, that was what mattered most, was it not? They could discuss all the finer details of their feelings and hopes for the future after the uproar of recent events settled down or were overwhelmed by the next tantalizing Society scandal.

"This one is lovely and sturdy, Mr. Harrowsmith," Lydia suggested, her voice monotone and her eyes fixed firmly on a few inches of thick lace she had pulled from a spool.

"Then I believe I have found the one. Good afternoon, Mrs. Dailey, Miss Dailey."

Sebastian dipped his head and hurried to the modiste with the spool of lace in hand. The perplexed woman took some convincing, suggesting a haberdashery instead, but she finally snipped several inches of lace and took a generous sum in return. As Sebastian scurried toward the front door, he spotted Lydia and her mother in the corner where they had been, examining fabrics on the wall, their backs to him. Mrs. Dailey's eyes flashed over her shoulder, unreadable.

Tucking the bit of lace into his coat pocket, Sebastian resumed the walk to his club, reaching into the pocket every once in a while to brush a finger against the material. Since little Christina did not actually care for lace in particular, especially not over her stuffed puppy, Sebastian did not see any harm in keeping it for himself, a token of his beloved to strengthen him during the uncertain days ahead.

"HIM? ENGAGED?" CRIED the acquaintance sitting across from Sebastian in the cozy gentlemen's club.

The man gawked at the newspaper sprawled before him that Sebastian had just handed over. A few others he knew to varying degrees chuckled and shook their heads.

"I never would have guessed Johnston of all people to finally shackle himself," said Shaw as he flipped the newspaper shut and dropped it on the side table laden with empty glasses.

"She is *handsomely* rich, or so I have heard from my sisters," Lord Gloverfield added from the nearby card table. The ruby signet ring on his little finger flashed in the candlelight as he leaned back in his chair and crossed his arms, a thick brow raised. "Apparently, there is an amount that can tempt even Johnston."

"That is why he goes to Boodle's and not Brooks's or White's." Shaw barked a laugh and ran a palm over his artfully shaped curls, held in place by much pomade.

Sebastian feigned a smirk as he sipped his coffee. All this gentlemanly conversation about bets and last winter's hunt and who belonged to which inferior clubs had grown tiresome. He looked down at the black coffee in his cup, swirling it.

Only Lydia's conversation had never grown tiresome, even when they fell into silence. There was still something spoken there, a mutual comfort that transcended words, at least any Sebastian could describe. Surely, Lydia would find just the right way to phrase it, shaped by her sharp wit and deep insight.

"What about you fellows? Have any of you been tempted out of the marriage mart and into matrimony?" Gloverfield asked as he smacked down a card.

Sinking lower in his chair, Sebastian busied himself with refilling his nearly full cup. He did not want prying gazes to remember his existence. In truth, he never spoke much when he came to Brooks's. Most of his friends from Bainbridge belonged to the highly exclusive White's. Yet it remained necessary that he visit his club regularly and maintain at least casual relationships with the other members to maintain good standing in Society—a necessary evil, as Lydia often put it.

"You know, I find myself pleasantly surprised by all that business at Lord Hammonton's ball earlier this week. Do you remember? Rigid and uninspiring Miss Dailey said all *that* to Lord Cleasehill? It was absurd to do so in public, but still, I cannot help admiring it," one gentleman rambled, gripping his chin in his hand.

Sebastian sank further still, his heart thudding against his lungs, a dull ache forming. He continued to sip his coffee and forced his unfocused eyes onto the corner of the newspaper he could see, ears hot.

"Can we really fault the lady?" another man called from the billiards table in the back of the room. "She merely said what we are all thinking. The viscount...." He shuddered, his cue sending the ball wide of its pocket. "I am glad he found the experience sufficiently embarrassing and is returning to the West Indies at the beginning of next week. At first, his stories were fascinating—until you realized they were all the same over and over again."

When Sebastian felt his head bobbing up and down in hearty agreement, he craned his neck toward the newspaper and redoubled his efforts to appear indifferent to their speculation.

Gloverfield scowled at the card table as he threw the remainder of his hand down. "That may be very true, indeed, I think we can all agree." The baron paused and a chorus of mumbles and nods answered. "In my opinion, Miss Dailey was very nearly on the shelf already and that display has solidified her position. I would never have peace with a wife like her, knowing she might speak to me so baldly at any moment. If she said such things to a man who is practically a stranger *and* her social superior, what might she say to the poor fool who marries her?"

Lead filled Sebastian's limbs. He glared at the corner of the newspaper, urging himself not to become entangled in their idle gossip. As much as he longed to come to Lydia's defense once more, he could not risk exposing the true nature of his feelings. Lydia already faced enough challenges without Sebastian earning her more of Mrs. Dailey's ire, which in turn would lead to further separation.

"She is not on *my* shelf," added a man from somewhere in the corner behind Sebastian writing a letter. "It certainly was not conventional, but I do admire someone who knows their worth."

"Goodness, no, not for me." Shaw waved a hand through the air, grimacing. "That single spark of liveliness cannot convince me that that marriage would not be just as dull as the vast majority of her presence amidst Society has been. Should a lady not smile at least once in her wretched life?"

Yet another voice chimed, dumping a bucket of ice water

over Sebastian's nearly boiling temper.

"Say whatever you like about Miss Dailey. I have already made my decision and spoken to my mama," announced Morris. The future baronet flashed a smile and lifted one shoulder in a shrug. "She will inform the lady and her family of my intentions to court her and arrange the necessary introduction. I, for one, would like to see if there are any other surprises under that frosty exterior. Besides, with a dowry so lavish, any lady would hoist her nose into the air at every opportunity. There must be good reason for her haughty disposition beyond wealth. Perhaps a little taming is all that is needed. My nature has always sought unique challenges."

"Well, why not ask Harrowsmith there?" Gloverfield jutted his chin in Sebastian's direction. Morris, seated opposite Sebastian in the loose circle of plush chairs, leaned forward, propping elbows on knees.

Sebastian forced his clenched fists to relax. It had taken all his willpower not to leap in brandishing a flaming sword in his beloved Lydia's defense. Now that they had involved him directly, Sebastian would not lie.

"It is your loss, all of you, for not considering that Miss Dailey might be a fascinating person who simply needs time to grow accustomed to someone before revealing it. Hard-won smiles can be immensely rewarding. They show the soul underneath the trained and tutored mask. Nor is she a challenge to be defeated."

All of the gentlemen in Brooks's fell into silence. Every eye turned to Sebastian, games and books and correspondence halted.

Sebastian sat straighter and met their surprised gazes with pride. He would gladly praise Lydia's virtues whenever the opportunity arose—especially if he could also defend her honor at the same time.

After a long moment of tension, Morris straightened in his chair and scoffed. "You must have won the race, then, eh, Harrowsmith?"

"Pardon?"

"You noticed the shifting tides of public perception and reached Miss Dailey before the rest of us. Of course you would have already asked to court her. It is an easy leap to make since you are already such dear friends."

Morris and a couple of other men, the ones who sided with the interested parties, shook their heads. They all happily employed underhanded methods to bolster their bets on card games, horse and carriage races, boxing matches, and any other inane wager they could find. Yet the thought of someone using an established connection to leverage himself into a lady's favor clearly disrespected the unspoken gentlemen's code by creating an unfair advantage.

Sebastian's head remained high as mumbles rippled through the dimly lit dark-paneled room. Finally, Gloverfield wrinkled his nose as his head dropped to one side, looking Sebastian up and down.

"Surely, she would have snatched up a friendly gentleman to spare herself the embarrassment of four, five Seasons on the marriage mart if she had any real interest. I suspect Miss Dailey is waiting for a man who is guaranteed to inherit his title. The current Baron Benning's surprise could very well be an heir. That would leave our dear Mr. Harrowsmith, well, Mr. Harrowsmith forevermore."

Embarrassment stung Sebastian's skin like embers. It was pathetic, really, to be made to feel ashamed of his lot. He had been nothing but grateful for the many luxuries his family enjoyed thanks to the comfortable wealth joined from both sides of his parents' marriage. He had been just as grateful as he had grown older and the reality had become clearer that his father would remain Lord Benning's heir. With Papa gone, Sebastian's position had been advanced, solidified. Or so they had assumed.

All the while, Lydia had never expressed any particular interest in titles—despite her mother's incessant influence. She had certainly never expressed anything short of happiness for Sebastian's fortunes without any judgements of his current uncertainty.

Yet that nagging thought that lurked like a dangerous undercurrent swelled to the surface once more, stronger for its recent absence. Gloverfield was correct. Lydia deserved more than Sebastian.

That thought had prevented him from trying to bridge the gap between his heart and Lydia's all these years. It had convinced him that Lydia would never see a possible future with him. He had watched it himself, the rigorous training she had undergone at Mrs. Dailey's insistence in order to attract the highest quality of gentlemen. Neither of them had seen that in lively, gregarious, plain Sebastian Harrowsmith. Lydia had only entertained the idea at Lady Swan's mysterious suggestion.

"Fear not, Harrowsmith," Gloverfield continued when Sebastian remained silent, lost in thought. "I am sure whoever manages to secure the Season's shocking novelty will allow you to write letters to her after she marries. We all know how fond you are of each other."

Sebastian rose and tugged on the lapels of his coat. "Then you understand why I felt the need to offer a different perspective on Ly—my friend."

"Come now, do not play coy! You must be courting her, Harrowsmith!"

Without acknowledging that last shout, Sebastian hastily bid the gentlemen farewell and quit Brooks's as quickly as his long legs would carry him. He was halfway down the twilight street, thundering past concerned passersby who had nothing but time on their hands to walk as slowly as they wished.

Time had never been a particularly kind companion to Sebastian. The more time passed, the more distant the possibility that his best friend would have a change of heart grew. He had come to assume that if Lydia had shown no romantic interest in him by now, she never would. Just like the men at Brooks's had said.

Time seemed to slip past too quickly for Sebastian to catch his breath. His head swam as he rounded the corner. He doubted even Lady Swan had intended for Lydia to draw quite so much attention to herself. Soon she would have curious gentlemen lining up at her family's door to beg the privilege of courting her.

Sebastian's fists clenched and unclenched at his sides as he marched toward home. Mama would be distressed at his sudden disinterest in joining her for a dinner party later that evening where Miss Woods would be in attendance, a fact she had dangled before him like a prize. Sebastian's only motivation in accepting had been the possibility of seeing Lydia there.

After the day he had had, after stealing a few moments to speak with her earlier, Sebastian felt no need to attend tonight. No, he needed to return home and stay there. After everything the others had said at Brooks's, Sebastian could not entertain the possibility of watching gentlemen swarm her for conversation, not when they were attracted to a curiosity rather than the real woman behind the much-discussed humbling of Viscount Cleasehill.

He had grown quite used to living with the undercurrent of anxiety in his stomach every time he saw Lydia dance or walk or ride with another gentleman. Though those instances typically only occurred once or twice with any one man, never approaching a proper courtship, Sebastian never knew if that man would be the one to catch her discerning eye. Knowing these men would be approaching Lydia starting with courtship at the forefront of their minds would be an agony all its own.

"Mr. Harrowsmith, welcome home—"

Sebastian stormed past the butler toward the stairs. Silence sliced through the ambient noise of London's streets as a footman swung the door closed behind him. Sebastian had not realized how much that noise had distracted him from the barrage of thoughts threatening to sweep him down a dangerous stream toward jagged rocks that would break him up against them if he could not find some way to keep his head above water.

The silence haunted Sebastian as he took the steps two at a time, boots thudding.

Leaning back on his closed door, Sebastian let his head thud against the wood. A twinge of strange discomfort that had been tugging at his mind reverberated with growing intensity as Sebastian's breath slowed.

Even when it seemed all his aching prayers had been answered, something prevented Sebastian from seeing his dreams to fruition. He pushed himself off the door and flopped unceremoniously face-first onto the bed. Half-smothered in a pillow, Sebastian felt around for another and dragged it over, clutching it to his chest.

How many times had he been on the verge of slipping, of saying something undeniable? He had already come dangerously close many times before. Over the course of their lives, Lydia had developed a keen ability to ignore Sebastian when he was being silly. It was her favorite word to describe him and Sebastian knew it, even if Lydia insisted that that in and of itself would be silly. She claimed her favorite word to describe him was the related yet far more refined "foolish."

Sebastian flipped onto his back and stretched his arms out wide, eyes tracing the artful geometry of moulding on the ceiling. He certainly felt foolish, his gut churning and skin stinging. How had the men at Brooks's known precisely what to say to stoke his insecurities and concerns for Lydia's best interests into this smoldering turmoil? It had felt so wonderful to be free of them while lost in memories of their kiss.

Shaking his head against the plush pile of pillows, Sebastian forced himself up. He shrugged out of his coat and draped it over his discarded boots. As he leaned back in the hopes of falling into a much-needed sleep, a flash of white caught his eye, peeking out from the pile of dark cloth.

Fast as lightning, Sebastian shot up and snatched the strip of lace out of his coat pocket. He cradled it in the palm of his hand, a smile twitching against his lips. Closing his fingers around it, he pressed his fist to his heart.

He had promised to wait. He had been devoted to Lydia his

entire life and he now had the privilege of devoting himself to her for the remainder of it. In the meantime, Sebastian resolved to do everything in his power to shed the burden of inferiority that weighed heavily on his heart. When the time finally came to bare his heart to Lydia, only the light and freedom she had always brought to his life would remain.

# CHAPTER FOURTEEN

L YDIA'S FINGERS DANCED across the pianoforte keys with the ease of hundreds of hours of practice. They did not betray an ounce of the embarrassment coiling in her stomach as footfalls thudded down the hall. Each perfect note floated into the air, Lydia's eyes fixed on the sheet music she had long since memorized. She needed time to brace herself.

"Mr. Harrowsmith," the butler announced, an arm stretched wide.

Lydia's fingers stumbled when Sebastian entered, hands behind his back and a curious smile gracing his handsome features. His eyes flew to her. So did Mother's. Lydia could feel them digging into the back of her head, forever searching for the root defect that, once located, could be eradicated once and for all.

"Welcome, Mr. Harrowsmith. So good of you to join us this afternoon."

Mother rose from her seat on the sofa in the middle of the drawing room. Lydia mirrored her, coming around to stand beside the instrument. Questions flitted across Sebastian's face as he looked from Lydia to her mother and back again. Lydia's heart lurched. She wished she could offer better answers than what he would soon receive.

"And I would also like to welcome you with great joy as Lydia's suitor."

There was no joy in the woman's voice. No welcome in her

eyes.

Sebastian's brow furrowed low over his tall nose, mouth pursing in that endearing expression of confusion. Lydia lowered her eyes to keep from glowering at her inability to enjoy it as it deserved. No amount of begging had convinced Mother to abandon this scheme.

"The two of you may take a turn about the room," Mother announced as she resumed her seat and took up her embroidery once more.

Sebastian offered his elbow to Lydia, just as he had done a hundred times before. Lydia's hand buzzed as she settled it on his forearm. She wanted nothing more than to let her head rest on his shoulder and sleep deeply for a good, long while.

"May I ask what your mother meant earlier?" Sebastian whispered, leaning down so his mouth brushed against Lydia's forehead when they looped around to the other side of the room.

Lydia took a deep breath, steeling herself, and stared straight ahead at the opposite wall. "I must confess that I have been receiving a surprising amount of positive attention from gentlemen in the past week since the ball."

Sebastian nodded quickly, his confused expression falling, as if he, too, did not wish to spend any more time on the topic than was necessary.

"Other ladies have been warmer as well, more welcoming. One told me yesterday that they were all glad I banished Lord Cleasehill across the sea before he could ensnare any of them."

"What you did was brave, Lydia," Sebastian agreed, his eyes softening around the corners. "You defended yourself and reminded others that they can do the same even if it is not proper, so long as it is right."

Lydia lowered her head, hoping that any shadows in the room would dull the heat of her blush. "It could very well have ruined my reputation. It is rather an odd turn that it hasn't.

"But there is more. Father heard from a friend who attends Brooks's that you apparently made known your intentions to court me. That is why Mother invited you today—to begin the courtship in earnest. She claims it will reflect poorly on me if a gentleman announces his intentions and rescinds them before the courtship even begins. That, in turn, could give other suitors reason to reconsider."

Sebastian grimaced at his shoes and shook his head. His other hand covered Lydia's where it rested on his arm and gave a comforting squeeze.

"I am sorry, Lydia. I am afraid those simpletons came to their own conclusions after a few of them took up the topic of your...*conversation* with Lord Cleasehill. A few of them did indeed express interest in making your acquaintance with the hopes of courting you. Apparently, the viscount is not a favorite amongst the gentlemen on this side of the sea, either. Naturally, knowing of our old friendship, they turned the question to me, but I only answered in order to defend you and quickly departed. They must have taken that as confirmation."

A comforting warmth eased the tension that had taken root in Lydia's body. She placed her other hand over the top of his. When he still did not look up, she prodded him in the ribs with her elbow. With a small smile, Sebastian lifted his head, guilt and shame writ large in his lovely eyes.

"Thank you for coming to my defense once more, my dear Sebastian," Lydia said quietly. Throwing a glance over her shoulder to ensure Mother's back was to them, Lydia let her head rest against Sebastian's shoulder for just a moment.

She had always secretly longed for someone who would understand and champion her, and she had had him in Sebastian all this time. When she lifted her head, the sun from the window illuminated a corner of the painting beside them where a pair of swans perched on the edge of a riverbank.

"What do you think of Lady Swan being correct after all?" Lydia asked. The more her focus had shifted to Sebastian, the less attention she had given to the mysterious letter that had started her Season with a wave of intrigue, the letter that had seemed so paramount to Lydia's happy ending. Neither of them had given the anonymous matchmaker so much as a passing word in recent days.

"Ah, yes—"

"Lord Brewsford and Mr. Sheppard!"

The butler's booming announcement jolted Lydia. She gripped Sebastian's forearm as her heartbeat skipped, the feeling reminiscent of taking the next step, only to find she'd run out of stairs. He patted her hand as he turned them to face the drawing room door, his expression suddenly unreadable.

"Sebastian?"

"Welcome, my lord, Mr. Sheppard. So good of you to join us today as Lydia's suitors." Mother beckoned to the gentlemen.

"Sebastian," Lydia hissed.

"Yes?"

The sad smile he offered her twisted Lydia's heart, but she did not have time to ponder it now. She would have to do something foreign to her nature until recently—act rashly.

"I know we have had scarcely a moment to ourselves to celebrate the wonders we have discovered, let alone discuss our desires for the future, but if you agree, I will reveal to my mother this very moment that I do not wish to accept these gentlemen as suitors…because I have you."

"Lydia, we have not even said—"

Checking once more that Mother and the other visitors enjoyed an engrossing conversation of family history and acquaintances, Lydia slipped her arm out of Sebastian's and grasped his hands.

"I know, but we will say it," Lydia promised. "For now, this is my only suggestion to rid us of—" She gestured toward the gentlemen and her mother.

Sebastian gave a hesitant nod. "If you are sure."

Lydia did not waste another moment. Turning on her heel, she crossed to the center of the drawing room. Her supposed suitors caught sight of her and lowered their heads respectfully.

"Here she is, my lovely daughter." Mother held up a hand before Lydia as if she were an item in a shop window.

"Good afternoon, my lord. Mr. Sheppard." Lydia curtseyed to the men, ignoring their anticipatory gazes, and rounded on her mother. "Might I request a private word?"

The woman's eyes sharpened. Lydia did not look away. "Very well. Gentlemen, perhaps you are acquainted with our other guest, Mr. Harrowsmith?" She nodded toward the wall, where Sebastian still lingered between two portraits of Dailey ancestors of old.

Lydia could feel Mother's stiff strides following behind her toward the far corner, her heart hammering with every step.

"What is this all about, Lydia? Should you be wasting any time when you have finally generated interest?"

"Mother, as you know, Sebastian wishes to court me," Lydia started. Her eyes darted over Mother's shoulder to the trio conversing on the opposite end of the room. Courage sparked in her chest when she spotted Sebastian, a loose, wavy lock draped over his forehead. It did not waver even when Mother's expression somehow managed to sour further.

"And because we have recently become aware of mutual affections, I have decided that he is the only suitor I desire. Please offer my sincerest apologies to Lord Brewsford and Mr. Sheppard."

Mother glowered at Lydia down her long nose. "I am afraid not."

"P-Pardon?" Lydia took a step back deeper into the corner.

"You may keep Mr. Harrowsmith as a suitor because his presence bolsters the appearance of demand, and that shall be the entirety of his usefulness to us."

Lydia's eyes widened in horror. "But, Mother, we lov—"

"I care not, Lydia!" Mother snapped. "You must accept the courtships of titled gentlemen or ones who are guaranteed to inherit, and you will choose from among them. I have long lamented my failure to act sooner on your behalf in the hopes that the skills I have raised you with would attract the right man. Yet just when I thought hope was lost, opportunity begins pouring in. You will not squander your chance as I did mine." As she spoke, the vein in her forehead slowly emerged, red and wrathful.

"They do not wish to marry me, Mother, none of them," Lydia pleaded under her breath, chest rising and falling rapidly. "They only want a chance to come near the latest Society spectacle, to see if I might embarrass myself for their entertainment. And you still insist on parading me out like some beast from the Royal Menagerie?"

Mother broke her gaze as the drawing room door swung open once more for a footman bearing a tea tray. "We have waited long enough. The opportunity is within our reach now. I will not allow you to waste this one, as you have wasted all the others. Go."

Shock hollowed Lydia's stomach as she caught Sebastian's gaze. She held up a hand and he obeyed, pausing while the other two men gathered on the chairs and accepted cups of tea from the footman. Lydia felt Mother's gaze on her back as she made her way back.

"What did she say?" Sebastian whispered, the corners of his mouth already angled down, as if he had read Lydia's thoughts from across the room.

"She said you may court me, but that I must allow whomever she deems worthy to also court me." Lydia turned her face away. She did not want Sebastian to see the darkness in her expression. "I have never seen her so determined to arrange a situation to her liking. Her own child's happiness is a worthy sacrifice in exchange for the improvement in our social standing. No, not *our* social standing. Hers. All because she is bitter that she was not able to secure a more advantageous marriage herself."

When Sebastian did not respond, Lydia dared a glance. The pain twisting his face sent a cold knife down her spine. Her fingers twitched, wanting nothing more than to reach out and take his hand, to comfort him. It was too risky now with the other gentlemen seated within view and Mother approaching from the other end.

"Seb—"

"Perhaps Mrs. Dailey is correct. At least as far as your options are concerned. Perhaps you should continue exploring, now that you have the opportunity. Lord Brewsford's estate boasts an entire floor dedicated to art, including several of your favorite artist's works."

Lydia's hands fell limp at her sides. She could only stare back, stunned into silence. Words tumbled through her head, evading her attempts to string them into a coherent sentence.

"Miss Dailey, Mr. Harrowsmith."

Mr. Sheppard, a future viscount, appeared in the corner of Lydia's eye, bearing two teacups. He offered one to her, which she accepted courteously. The other he kept for himself, cradling it in both hands as he glanced between the pair.

"I heard that you grew up together in Bainbridge. I am afraid to say I have never had the privilege of visiting the place. Tell me, what is Bainbridge like?"

All of Lydia's senses rushed back in full force, an idea forming on the tip of her tongue in an instant. She gave Sebastian a pointed look. "Bainbridge is my favorite place in the world. It has always been my home and it always will be."

Lydia's heart thundered with the force of her prayers that Sebastian would understand and find the reassurance he needed. They had nearly reached the end of their trials, she could feel it. They had come all this way—to an official courtship! They could not lose now.

"Not always, dear," Mother corrected. Her eyes did not blink as she took a slow sip of tea, but they were not looking at Lydia. They were looking at Sebastian.

# CHAPTER FIFTEEN

"**M**AIL FOR YOU, sir."

Sebastian looked up from his sliced ham at the footman's offered tray. A single letter sat in the center. He did not recognize the handwriting as that of any of his friends who rarely had the interest or time to write letters and his older sister communicated all her news to Mama, trusting she would happily relay it all.

"Thank you." Sebastian snatched the letter. He tried, unsuccessfully, to dismiss the feeling of eyes upon him as he broke the seal with a clean butter knife. Had Lady Swan decided to extend her help to him now that her entire plan—if this was indeed her plan—was in danger? The matchmaker had been silent since Lydia's second letter, which had been as vague as the first.

"Who is that from, dearest?" Mama chirped from the head of the table over her own generous stack of correspondence.

Sebastian's eyes trailed to the bottom of the letter. *Mrs. Dailey?*

"Well, would you look at that? A friend has returned from the Continent with many stories to share."

Mama nodded and returned to her own mail. Nerves churned in Sebastian's stomach as he forced his eyes back to the beginning. He doubted Lydia's mother contacting him directly could lead to anything good.

Sebastian's frown deepened as he read the sparse paragraphs.

Did all ladies with their minds set on matchmaking write letters this abstract? The only thing Mrs. Dailey would divulge was her ardent wish that Sebastian return to their home today to continue their discussion.

They had not discussed much yesterday outside of her sudden welcome of Sebastian as a suitor. His stomach twisted around itself painfully. No, he did not like this at all. Yet he must accept her summons.

All too soon, Sebastian found himself back on the Daileys' doorstep. Their butler led him not up the stairs to the drawing room but straight down the hall toward the back of the townhouse. A pair of waiting footmen opened the double doors at his approach and he stepped into a modest back garden. Sebastian could feel something in the very air constricting him, like a trap slowly springing.

Mrs. Dailey sat at a small table in the far corner under the shade of an awning. She met Sebastian's gaze, a silent command to come forth. The polite cough of the footman lingering in the doorway at his back prodded Sebastian from behind. He crossed the well-kept grass, the footman racing past him with tea tray in hand, and bowed to Lydia's mother.

"Thank you for coming, Mr. Harrowsmith, both today and yesterday," the lady began as she dismissed the footman and poured their tea.

"Of course." Sebastian nodded. "It is always my pleasure to come when the Dailey house calls."

Eyes like Lydia's in color but devoid of all her heart narrowed at Sebastian, waiting until he finished his sip, demanding full attention. "I hope you know that I consider your admiration of my daughter to be the highest compliment."

Sebastian set the cup down on its saucer, the tea suddenly tasting bitter.

"Your interest in courting her is much appreciated, certainly," Mrs. Dailey continued, her teacup hovering in her dainty grip. "I had hoped things would continue as always, your friendship with my daughter not unappreciated, but now that is not to be the case, I must deliver a difficult truth to you, sir. You see, I have tirelessly guided Lydia away from the unfortunate tenuous fact of your inheritance toward those with assured titles. What I could not achieve in my time, I must ensure Lydia does. You must understand how vital it is for a mother to secure the absolute best for her child's happiness and wellbeing. Now that your uncle has been blessed with a potential heir, you must see that your situation simply cannot breed confidence."

The sneers from the gentlemen's club rushed to the front of Sebastian's mind. It was his turn to glare as Mrs. Dailey finally indulged in a sip. "Tell me, madam, have you shared those sentiments with anyone else recently?"

Mrs. Dailey looked down into her cup, bonnet covering her face. "Mothers of the *ton* discuss so many things, it is impossible to remember it all."

Sebastian nodded slowly. It confirmed his suspicions. It was meant to. No matter how comfortable a life Sebastian could provide, it would never be enough without "Lord" before his name. Mrs. Dailey had been solidifying that message in both his and Lydia's souls since they'd been children, finding subtle ways to emphasize the difference in Sebastian's uncertain future and Lydia's, full of promise.

"Mr. Harrowsmith," Mrs. Dailey continued, "if you love Lydia, whether as a sweetheart or a friend, I urge you to do what is best for her and remove yourself from her consideration. I shall not extinguish your friendship, however, if either of you care to maintain it. That is of no concern to me. You see, she is at the precipice of finally taking the place in Society that she has been denied because no one appreciates the value of true perfection when they see it. Once Lydia has the promise of a title, her circle of influential connections will extend beyond her little Bainbridge group."

Sebastian's blood turned to ice. Mrs. Dailey had just proven her daughter's fears correct. The woman saw Lydia as nothing more than a means to advance her own position in Society. Her cool eyes glinted in the shade as she dared Sebastian to challenge her.

Dozens of choice words raced to his lips, not the least of which was the fact that Mrs. Dailey was the very reason Lydia struggled to feel at ease around others, the very reason she presented an impenetrable wall to the rest of the world. The poor creature lived in constant fear of offending someone and further distancing herself from the unfairly conditional love she so earnestly desired.

It took every ounce of strength Sebastian had not to throw all the damage Mrs. Dailey had done to her own child in the woman's face. As a gentleman, he still had a duty to maintain a certain level of politeness and restraint around ladies. Sebastian's words would be ringing through this entire row of gardens had he been contending with Mr. Dailey instead. Most importantly of all, Sebastian would not give Lydia's mother any more reason to increase the difficulties in his beloved's life.

"Let me ask you this," Mrs. Dailey continued after several long moments of silence punctuated only by the occasional light sip of tea. "And I do hope you will forgive me for this terrible bluntness, but do you truly, truly think you are worthy of my Lydia?"

The whispered words, more threat than question, hung in the warm, spring air. Sebastian's feet fell out from under him, his stomach a tempestuous mess. His greatest insecurity had been laid bare before him, twisted to suit Mrs. Dailey's foul plan. He gritted his teeth, fists clenched atop his knees.

"If for some laughable reason, you think you do," Mrs. Dailey continued over the rim of her teacup, "I encourage you to closely examine the gentlemen who will be courting her now. See if you measure up then."

"And if *Lydia* does not care for such considerations?" Sebastian challenged through gritted teeth, emphasizing her given name. The words sounded hollow in his own ears for the blood rushing through them.

Mrs. Dailey's eyes darkened. "She will. At least, she will when she hears whispers behind her back of how Mr. Harrowsmith followed her into a dark hallway to steal a kiss. Her reputation would never recover, even if you did race off to Gretna Green under cover of darkness. But really, it need not come to all that. You would not allow such a thing, would you?"

# CHAPTER SIXTEEN

"YOU WOULD NOT *allow such a thing, would you?"*

Mrs. Dailey's words continued to haunt Sebastian's mind as he trudged up the steps to the Theatre Royale the following day. The entire conversation echoed over and over again under the surface of his every thought. He had not been able to taste tea since.

Nor had he been able to determine exactly how Mrs. Dailey knew. Surely, Lydia would not have dared confess unless under extreme pressure. Sebastian hated to think of her in such a position. Had a servant reported their indiscretion? Who else might have seen and might be drafting a tantalizing piece for the scandal sheets?

Mama, one of his younger brothers, and his sister and brother-in-law paused in the grand foyer under the light of the ornate brass and crystal chandelier. The two ladies conducted the necessary examination of the room for any familiar faces of note. As the finest members of the *ton* filtered around them, weighted with jewels and waving luxurious fans to dispel the heat of so many bodies, Sebastian vaguely wondered how they could simper and giggle and joyfully anticipate this lauded performance of *Richard III* while his world slipped through his fingers with every passing moment and he was entirely powerless to stop it.

Should he heed Mrs. Dailey's bald threat to remove his name from the list of Lydia's suitors, to erase their kiss from the records, and claim it had been a mistake to extend their friendship beyond its natural bounds? To see if there was any way they could return to who they had been before the kiss, before the Season, before Lady Swan's letter?

Something clutched Sebastian's chest and squeezed the air from his lungs. He had no choice. Not with Lydia's good standing in the world at risk. He knew well enough that if a lady lost that, she lost everything. And if she did, it would be entirely his fault. He was the one who had ignored the shadows and kissed her.

Worse still, Sebastian hated the part of himself that hoped Mrs. Dailey was right. It was the cowardly way out of a future where he would be forced to confront his shortcomings even more acutely on a daily basis. Lydia certainly deserved a man braver than that. Perhaps a retreat was the bravest option left to Sebastian now.

"Sebastian?" Mama called, voice muffled by the growing crowd. "I swear, your mind has been lost to the clouds recently."

Shaking his head, Sebastian desperately tried to cloak those thoughts with the normalcy surrounding him. It was the only way he would make it through the night. Despite his generous height, Sebastian did not spy the others until lifting himself onto his toes to see above bejeweled heads and perfectly styled coiffures.

"Coming, Mama!" he replied as he began the arduous process of weaving through the crowd toward the side doors, throwing out murmured apologies along the way.

"Seb—!"

Sebastian whirled around just as he broke through the final cluster of theater-goers. Even Lydia's voice followed him like a ghost. The lovely lilt and rich tones that colored so many of his most precious memories only served to deepen the jagged pit that had been growing in his heart.

Mama clicked her tongue, growing impatient, and nodded to her eldest child. Ever the dutiful daughter, Sebastian's sister grabbed his wrist and tugged him behind them through the opulent carved and painted doors, their younger brother snickering into his ostentatiously puffed cravat. Wrinkling his nose, Sebastian landed a soft punch against the lad's lower back as they shuffled into their box.

They had only been seated a few minutes, the boxes around them filling quickly as the first act approached, when Sebastian's hopes of a mental escape into drama were dashed.

"Sebastian? Is that not Miss Dailey all the way up there?"

He forced his nervous eyes to dart up and to the left. Instantly, his gaze found her, as if he somehow always knew where she was.

Lydia sat at the very front of one of the best boxes in the theater. Perfectly centered and draped in fine, red velvet, it afforded the clearest view enjoyed in the finest luxury. She glowed in a beautiful gown of blush, dotted with diamonds and pearls, dark hair piled in intricate loops. A gentleman Sebastian knew only by sight whispered something in Lydia's ear that inspired a small smile.

"Yes, that is Miss Dailey," Sebastian mumbled. "Tell me, how are Dorothy and Christina?" He redirected his sister's attention to the ever-popular topic of her daughters, for once hoping Lydia would not find him in the crowd.

Most of his sister's proud anecdotes of the girls' recent antics drifted in one ear and out the other as Sebastian tried not to think about how ethereal and perfect Lydia looked up there. Like the other ladies in her box, Lydia's immaculate dignity and grace held her apart from everyone else. They possessed an ease of movement borne of their natural stations as daughters of lords. Sebastian had no doubt Lydia would quickly adopt the true effortlessness of their manners with enough time in their elevated company.

Mrs. Dailey's rigorous upbringing had indeed molded Lydia into the perfect ladylike shape to join those lofty ranks. Who was Sebastian to deny her that, especially after he'd nearly ruined her?

"Christina has been fussing more at night when it is time for sleep and she will throw dreadful tantrums if you attempt to dress her in the incorrect outfit—Oh, Mr. and Mrs. Baker are here, and just in time!"

Sebastian bit down on the inside of his cheek. The last thing he needed was a few stragglers slinking into their box and drawing a particular pair of eyes his way. He and the other seated gentlemen rose and greeted the newcomers sharing their box for the evening.

A faint swish of pink caught Sebastian's attention as he resumed his seat. His eyes trailed upward past several levels of boxes. Lydia's smile dazzled him across the theater, a silken hand offering a small wave. The earl beside her glanced in Sebastian's direction and whispered in Lydia's ear again.

Even from here, Sebastian could see the shape of his name on her lips, so familiar and natural. Ignoring the cold ache in his chest, Sebastian forced a hand up, keeping it tight to his body, and returned a fraction of her smile.

His eyes remained on Lydia as the audience hushed and the curtains swept open. She nodded to her companion and pointed to something on her playbill. A sickly feeling rippled through Sebastian's stomach as he wondered if he was looking at a vision of his future—Lydia up there in the light, surrounded by Society's finest, while he remained down below, watching from a plain, off-center box. The secret of their kiss would remain tucked away in a hidden corner of his chest, never to see the surface again. He would protect Lydia with his silence.

By the time Sebastian had emerged onto the pavement outside the theater, a sea of London's finest spilling out behind him, the play had already faded from his memory as if he had watched it through a mist. He could hardly remember all the other rambling thoughts that had occupied his mind for the past several hours.

None of them had been remotely helpful in guiding Sebastian out of this web in a way that could secure both his and Lydia's happiness. Even if Lydia claimed she cared not for titles or the fact that her own mother had threatened to ruin her reputation if she stepped any further out of line, Mrs. Dailey had been correct about one thing. Sebastian would not allow that to happen. There was no way to know if her mother would stand by her spiteful promise. The consequences of a life forever on the outskirts of Society were colder and crueler than they could yet imagine.

His aching heart pulsed with the certainty of what he must do.

Only Sebastian and Mama occupied the carriage on the ride home. His sister and brother-in-law had arrived in their own carriage and his brother had opted to extend the evening in a friend's parlor. Sebastian pressed his back into the cushions of his seat, Mama gazing sleepily out the window. He had been counting on his brother's presence to dissuade him from blurting out a certain question, one only Mama could answer.

It was a question that would unexpectedly populate in the corner of his mind over the years, easily dismissed by the truths Sebastian had thought so certain until recently. It had been itching on his mind and in his mouth since his disastrous meeting with Mrs. Dailey.

Now that he found himself with a private moment with his mother, Sebastian's fraying control snapped.

"Mama, have you ever thought that Lydia and I suited each other?"

Her head spun around. "Well, in truth, no," she admitted thoughtfully. "Only because Lydia is so formal and severe, not unlike her mother, I am afraid to say. You would do better with a mirthful little thing, do not you think? A girl who recognizes humor, someone you can make laugh. You do love to make others laugh, my dear boy."

It was Sebastian's turn to look pensively out the window. Reflected in the glass he saw Lydia's smile when she laughed. Of course Mama had never been privileged to be in Lydia's company during those rare times when she lowered her guard. She reserved that only for Sebastian and their Bainbridge friends.

Sebastian could make her laugh. He could make her laugh better than anyone else. She felt free with him. Couldn't that be enough?

Mama cleared her throat. When Sebastian glanced in her direction he found her expression serious and a touch sheepish. "Of course it seems all the attention on Miss Dailey has only reinforced her mother's desire to seek matches with titles."

The older woman's cheeks tinged and she smiled ruefully at her hands folded neatly in her emerald skirts. Sebastian's jaw clenched as he once more thought of Mrs. Dailey's complete lack of regard for those she professed to care for.

His mother had been blindsided and heartbroken by two life-changing losses—the death of her husband and the miraculous news of her brother-in-law's long-awaited child, potentially forcing her own son further down the line for the barony.

Mrs. Dailey's parading of her belief that untitled gentlemen were inadequate matches for her daughter only reminded Mama of the opportunities her son had lost. Though Sebastian could never truly be free of that fact, his mother did her best to distract herself from the scars left by grief and crushing disappointment.

"That does exclude you, I am afraid, even if Mrs. Dailey says she is allowing you to court her daughter for appearances," Mama added with a listless lift of one shoulder. "Goodness, after all these years, you have not suddenly taken an interest, have you?" She chuckled, waving her closed fan at the far-fetched idea. "What miserable timing that would be."

"Miserable, indeed," Sebastian agreed through gritted teeth.

He returned his gaze to the shadowy streets beyond the window dipping in and out of view in time to the horses' clopping hooves, praying Mama would sense the end of the conversation. No one need remind him that the whole of England could see he would never be Lydia's equal. Everyone knew that but him, no matter how hard he tried to fool himself into believing that he'd accepted the truth.

"Ah, that reminds me," Mama chirped. "I have not yet had an

opportunity to ask what you thought of our luncheon earlier today!"

"Luncheon?"

"I swear, you young men lose yourselves in flights of fancy as much as the young misses. Yes, the luncheon, Sebastian. With Miss Woods and her delightful parents?"

Sebastian squeezed his eyes shut, a finger drilling an incessant beat against his knee. "Ah, indeed. And the Rose and Atkinson families as well. All exceedingly charming guests."

Mama's subtle and occasional prodding had grown more persistent throughout the Season, especially now that her dear friend Mrs. Dailey looked on the verge of having her choice of advantageous and handsome matches for her child. Apparently, that now included erasing their other guests from Sebastian's memory if that would concentrate his focus on her chosen Miss Woods.

"Certainly! I am so thrilled you agree." Mama pressed a hand to her chest, eyes alight, as if Sebastian had singled out the Woodses specifically. "Did you hear Miss Woods on the pianoforte? A talent like I have never seen on that odious instrument! You know how I always detest having to play it. Of course I prefer singing, and Miss Woods says she is quite accomplished there as well. Naturally! We shall have to arrange a gathering to hear her sing...."

Mama contented herself with extolling Miss Woods's virtues to an unwilling audience, oblivious to Sebastian's lack of participation. Sebastian substituted one unwanted discourse for another, drowning out his mother's praises of another woman with his own self-interrogation founded upon one question.

Would Sebastian have the strength to let go of Lydia after coming so wonderfully close to having her?

When he believed with every fiber of his being that Lydia deserved the world, how could Sebastian ever think himself worthy of giving it to her? Clearly, everyone else had seen a deficiency from the start—even Lydia herself. If Lady Swan had never written, perhaps Lydia would have never considered Sebastian of her own volition. Sebastian had been the only one clinging to that scrap of delusional hope that she might one day change a mind that had always known better than his.

By the time they arrived at their townhouse, just a street away from Lydia's, Sebastian was no closer to any of the answers his foolish heart sought.

# CHAPTER SEVENTEEN

LYDIA BRUSHED HER hands down the front of her pastel-yellow evening gown and tugged at the tops of her silk gloves as the footman opened Mother's sitting room door. Mother always liked a private viewing of Lydia's dress, accessories, and hair before any event, a nerve-wracking necessity every time.

Unfortunately, Lydia had already earned her mother's ire because the modiste had been unable to finish her new gown on time, leaving Lydia to wear her next-newest one. Mother cared not that it was no fault of Lydia's, only that something involving her had gone wrong.

"Well," Mother snipped when Lydia strode to the center of the floral rug and took her usual place. She looked her daughter up and down, expression unreadable. "Presentable indeed."

Lydia held her breath. "'Indeed'?" The addition of that word made an unusually generous compliment. Of course Mother herself was the epitome of steely beauty in her azure gown, her eyes honing in on every detail of Lydia's ensemble in turn, forever searching for defects.

"Yes, now stop mimicking me. It is unseemly. You will do well. I suspect a few new courtships will bloom tonight. Including another involving your old friend Mr. Harrowsmith, if the rumors are to be believed."

Lydia's fragile heart slammed into a brick wall. She turned her back to Mother and crossed to the vanity on the wall, feigning interest in her own reflection. "What rumors are those?"

"He has not told you himself? I am surprised," Mother mused from her chaise lounge. "It seems you are not the only possibility in his sights. In fact, Mrs. Harrowsmith speaks with great certainty of mutual interest between her son and Miss Woods."

Keeping her unfocused eyes on the blurry glass as she absentmindedly adjusted her necklace, Lydia nodded and clenched her teeth against the shameful doubt creeping up along her spine. London was rife with rumors, miscommunications, and hopes destined to be dashed.

"And I must say, having seen them together on a number of occasions this Season, I ardently agree with Mrs. Harrowsmith that the pair is perfectly suited," Mother continued, plucking up vials with smelling salts, perfumes, and creams from the table beside her and stowing them in her reticule. "Such a bright, young man must be matched with a lady of spirit. Anything else would be an injustice, do not you agree, Lydia? Still, it was quite thoughtful of him to offer himself up as your suitor to enhance your appeal."

Straightening her spine, back still to her mother, Lydia used all the willpower she could muster to etch a polite smile onto her face. She turned.

"I certainly do agree, Mother."

Mother rose from the lounge that Lydia doubted had ever been properly lounged upon and joined her before the vanity. Lydia lowered her eyes as the woman fussed with the curls framing her face, the ministrations gentle yet devoid of tenderness.

"B-But...." The word fell out of Lydia's mouth before she could stop herself.

Standing at her back, Mother scowled at Lydia through the glass. "Do not mumble. Speak with conviction."

Lydia stood a little taller. Hadn't Mother been scolding her for speaking with conviction just a week ago? "But the other day, when you made him a suitor—"

"Did I not tell you?" A strange emotion flickered in the woman's eyes as she turned away, something like…satisfaction. "Dear Mr. Harrowsmith called upon me the very next day and apologized profusely for rescinding his name from your consideration so soon. I thought it would be better for you to wait to hear the official proclamation directly from your friend, but since you insist on forcing yourself where you do not belong…."

Lydia's ears burned. What on Earth was she hearing right now? It could not be possible. It could not be possible that Sebastian would kiss and court her one day and propose to Miss Woods the next. Her Sebastian would never do something so heartless.

"It appears whatever conflict there was between Mr. Harrowsmith and Miss Woods has been happily resolved. Something about confused feelings."

Lydia's limbs felt weightless, translucent. Her stomach sank down to her feet, her heart flittering at a dizzying pace in the space where her vanished brain had been. It could not be. Yet she could not deny that it very well could. Of course it had come back to Miss Woods. She was the early favorite, the obvious choice. She had certainly won over the woman who would be her mother-in-law.

"He will be so happy now that he has realized what he wants, I am sure of it. And how happy it must make a dear friend to support another in their happiness, yes?"

Head spinning, Lydia nodded again, too shocked for tears. She accepted Mother's hand and allowed herself to be led out of the finely furnished sitting room and down to the ballroom, where their male relations awaited. As her family stepped into the glittering, bustling room, she prayed with all her might that she would hold her breaking heart together long enough to survive this night.

The world ground to a halt as Lydia's traitorous eyes immediately landed upon none other than Miss Woods. The lady, wearing a beautiful ivory gown with silver overlays, chatted with her parents at the edge of the dance floor near the musicians. Lydia did not dare to glance at her mother. Would a word of warning have been too much to ask?

A modicum of relief punctuated Lydia's miserable haze when a familiar pair of blonde heads bobbing through the guests stole her attention from the presence of the woman who had won a race Lydia had begun far too late. Felicity and Mercy appeared at Lydia's side, the other girls trailing behind.

"Remember, fill your card or I will fill it for you," Mother commanded under her breath without removing her gaze from the already impressive gathering of guests, her voice trailing away as she followed behind Father to begin the festivities.

The threat trickled down Lydia's spine like melting ice. Isabel and Clara each looped an arm around one of hers, combating the aftereffects of her mother's glacial presence. For once, Lydia allowed herself to lean into her friends' support. Moments ago, she had felt as though she were falling endlessly through thin air. Now stones filled her limbs and sat atop her chest, on the verge of crushing her, dragging her under.

Leading them in a single-file line, Mercy wove around groups of eager guests waiting for the dancing to begin toward a vacant spot along the wall. Felicity wasted no time in sneaking strawberries off the artful fruit tower as everyone huddled in close around Lydia.

"Lydia, we just overheard something dreadful," Isabel began, grasping her hand. "Apparently, Mrs. Gardiner told my Aunt Matilda that she heard Mr. Harrowsmith has been courting Miss Woods in secret this entire Season and will soon be ready to reveal their affections after he proposes."

Steady hands gripped her elbows, her friends' murmured words arriving at her ears through a long tunnel. Why was she surprised? It all made sense. Everything Mother had said earlier in her sitting room made sense. Miss Woods made sense for Sebastian.

"Oh, darling, are you unwell?"

"Would you like something to drink?"

Her friends' concerned questions all received a listless shake of the head. For now, none of that mattered in this state of limbo as the inevitable sank into her bones.

She supposed the real shock came from the fact that every person in London had heard of it before her. Sebastian was her best friend. Surely, he would have told her his interests were engaged. Had Lydia known that when Lady Swan's letter had arrived, she might have spared them both the confusing mess by never exposing her mind to that possibility…to *his* possibility, to all the happiness he promised.

No, that happiness had never been meant for her. It was meant for Miss Woods.

Thanks to Lady Swan's meddling and Lydia's naivety, Sebastian had mistaken his flourishing feelings for Miss Woods with his deep affections for his oldest friend. And to think Lydia had nearly caused him to miss his true path to joyful matrimony. The word "joy" had never suited Lydia.

"Come, why don't you sit?" Ellen suggested softly, a hand on the small of Lydia's back.

At that, Lydia nodded. Her knees suddenly felt untrustworthy. The others formed a protective circle around Lydia as Ellen guided her toward the nearest chair. The ballroom came to life all around them with guests mingling and filling themselves with refreshments ahead of a long night of dancing.

Lydia sank into the seat with a sigh, never allowing her spine to bend. Several hands appeared before her face bearing handkerchiefs and glasses of punch and plates of all manner of treats. Frowning, she waved them all away.

"I am just a little winded. I need a moment, that is all."

Her friends stepped aside. Lydia's eyes fell on the double doors straight across the room as two footmen pushed them open from the other side. Her throat constricted as Sebastian and the rest of the Harrowsmiths entered.

"Look!" Clara gasped, mouth agape.

Lydia did not need to look. As always, she instinctively knew where Sebastian was, even when she did not want to. Their eyes met across the ballroom. Lydia could see the desire to speak building behind his expression. Her heart longed to answer while her mind wanted nothing more than to cower in a dark corner, hidden away from the inevitable conversation.

Reaching up, Mrs. Harrowsmith grasped both of Sebastian's shoulders and turned him, giving him a light push in her chosen direction—straight toward the Woods family. Though Lydia's friends valiantly encircled her once more, the empty spaces between their silhouettes still afforded Lydia enough of a view as the handsome pair took to the dance floor with several other couples to open the ball.

"Mercy, Felicity, there you are!" The Viscountess Eldmar's harried hiss surprised them all. The woman stormed toward them from the opposite corner, dripping in extravagance.

"Go," Lydia urged, pushing the twins toward their mother. "Attend to your own demands. I can manage mine."

"Isabel, finally, could you locate your aunt for me?" said Isabel's father, a portly man with a kind, rosy complexion, from their other side. He held up a small bauble pinched between his fingers, glinting in the candlelight. "I just realized my other cufflink has gone missing and I hoped she might have thought to take along an extra set in her reticule."

"Go," Lydia said once more, this time with a strained chuckle. "Enjoy your evenings. I expect detailed and fascinating reports at our next meeting. And do not think I will not grade you harshly for a lackluster report simply because you spent the entire night coddling me."

After one more heartfelt inquiry from Ellen, the girls dispersed throughout the ballroom, always balancing the tightrope between their friends' dramas, their guardians' whims, and their own desires. Lydia watched them go and wished them all well. They need not absorb her sorrow and miss their own chances.

Not a minute later, Lydia watched a handful of gentlemen

notice her sitting alone by the wall and approach. She did her best to calm her frayed mind and confused heart. Whatever she felt on the inside, even if she felt as though she were crumbling bit by bit, she still owed these men a proper greeting and conversation.

"Miss Dailey, good evening! What a miracle we were able to find you amidst this chaos," said the one at the front, a future baron Lydia had met at a dinner just two days ago.

"A miracle, indeed," Lydia agreed, a touch too monotone, as her eyes disobeyed her and surveyed the room for Sebastian. He and Miss Woods twirled in perfect time, sharing a seemingly fascinating conversation that inspired delightful giggles in the lady.

"Are you looking for someone, Miss Dailey?" another gentleman prodded, glancing over his shoulder.

Lydia shook her head lightly, the curls at the nape of her neck swishing. "Forgive me. If I appear to be absentminded tonight, it is only because my parents look to me to assist when they host events."

Her new companions nodded understandingly. "Of course," yet another added. "A noble endeavor, and I pray you will accept my praises and repeat them to your parents. Though it is early, I declare the night a resounding success already!"

The others agreed heartily, their own flowery compliments intermingling in their attempts to stand out for her. For *her*. When was the last time she had dreamed of a single suitor tripping over himself to win her affections, let alone this many? Not since her first Season, no doubt. That simple dream had been quickly tempered by reality. Now she did not want any one of these gentlemen, disguising their curiosity with Society's latest fascination as an interest in courtship.

"Thank you all. That is wonderfully generous. My parents will be overjoyed to know you are already enjoying yourselves so thoroughly," Lydia said, snapping her fan open and waving it before her face, blurring the distant figures of Sebastian and Miss Woods in her peripheral vision.

"Miss Dailey," said a future viscount Lydia had met at a luncheon yesterday, edging his way to the front of her bristling mob. "I would love an opportunity to continue our conversation about the painting masters. May I have the next dance?"

A chorus of similar requests rang through Lydia's ears as the other gentlemen seized the opening, the competitive side of their chivalry urging them to courteously fight for their place on a lady's dance card. When all was said and done and they finally dispersed to try their chances with the other eligible misses in attendance, the entire front side of Lydia's card had been filled. Once one of them had the idea to claim two dances from the start, the others had scrambled to do the same, never to be outdone.

Lydia looked down at the unfamiliar card. She had never seen so many different names on one of hers. A hollow feeling worried away at her stomach, though she had been so busy throughout the day with morning engagements and preparing for the ball that she hadn't eaten since breakfast.

To her relief, no one else approached her for a long while, her parents' many friends and acquaintances shuffling by to the sideboard for fruits and cheeses or to greet another guest as the first dance came to a crescendo. She numbly marveled that she was not glad for this sudden turn in her luck after years of hoping for so much as a lingering glance, all the while watching Sebastian smiling and laughing with a lady who looked as though she belonged with him.

Lydia welcomed the forced reprieve from her melancholy thoughts when the first gentleman came to claim his dance. That would not have been the case if Sebastian had remained on the floor to participate in the next set. She would have had to dance portions of it with him, and she had not yet had sufficient opportunity to gather her thoughts, soothe her unjustly injured feelings, and create a defense to face him. Not when they must stand so close, one hand on her waist and the other grasping hers, firm yet gentle—

The hand holding hers squeezed tight as the first formation began. Lydia jolted and looked up. Green eyes stared back instead of deep brown. His smile did not reach the corners of his eyes. That was right. She danced with some other man, not Sebastian.

Even now, despite what her anguished mind knew, Lydia would rather have been in Sebastian's arms. Perhaps that was why she had never been truly distraught at her lack of dances, why she had never put forth more effort into endearing gentlemen to her—because she had never truly sought other gentlemen. Sebastian had been everything Lydia had wanted and needed without her realizing it. She had realized it too late.

Who was she to stand between her dearest friend and his chance at true happiness? Lydia would have never forgiven herself if she had. Especially when it was her fault that Lady Swan's inane letter had muddled his thoughts and encouraged him to feel affections that did not truly belong to him.

"I trust you are having an enjoyable evening, Miss Dailey?" her partner started, dragging Lydia away from those dangerous places in the dark corners of her heart. She need not visit now, not in the middle of a ball.

Mother had trained her for this. The flawless outer shell could hide tempests. Not a single other soul would know. Ladies were meant to experience emotions, but not real ones. They were meant to swoon and flutter and balance on the verge of offense over innocuous things. Any deeper feeling remained behind the shell. This was expected of all ladies, Mother had made that clear, yet even more so for *ladies* who represented their husbands' titles and proud family histories.

"Most enjoyable," Lydia lied, molding her lips into a smile. "Tell me, how has your Season been thus far?"

Several dances passed in much the same way. Lydia used every opportunity to turn broad questions with potential for meandering answers to her partners. Speaking took more energy than she could expend, yet listening to the gentlemen's stories of brave hunts and favorite philosophers and the many luxuries of their estates kept her mind engaged, safely tethered to the present moment. Away from Sebastian.

"May I fetch you a refreshment, Miss Dailey?" asked Lord Flemingwell as he led her off the dance floor.

She nodded, intent on sending him away when he returned, claiming a dizzy spell. That always bought a moment. She did indeed need a moment, but not with him. The young viscount hurried away. Feet pulsing in her suddenly constricting slippers, Lydia did her best to gracefully shuffle toward the nearest chair.

"Lydia, finally."

The ache in her limbs instantly vanished. Lydia whirled around. Sebastian stood with a hand outstretched, a strange expression on his face, what she could only describe as *pained*. Guilty, perhaps. Lydia straightened her spine and sealed the cracks forming in her heart as best she could. She had hoped to delay this for a while, yet she would face it if she must. Besides, she must let Sebastian know he had no cause for guilt. Any guilt was hers to bear.

"Good evening, Sebastian."

"I hoped to speak with you."

"Please do."

"It is a bit…." Sebastian glanced from side to side sheepishly.

"Crowded?" Lydia finished, fighting an instinctual smile. Even now, when she knew what was about to happen—what *must* happen—she could not stop herself from finding her best friend entirely charming and maddeningly handsome. She could not stop herself from glancing at his wonderful, sweet mouth that would haunt her for the remainder of her days.

Would anything have changed if she'd noticed it before? If she'd truly appreciated his kind, steadfast, lighthearted presence in her life? She knew the truth of her love now, and he still did not want her.

Sebastian chuckled under his breath and offered his arm to Lydia. Her chest tightened as she accepted, forcing her gaze into the distance at the feathery contraption atop Lady Eldmar's fashionable curls. Anywhere but that enchanting half-smile.

He led her slowly, his gaze darting to the exquisitely embroidered hem of her gown and the matching slippers peeping out with every step. The confirmation of his notice and care to not walk too fast for her sore feet only forced Lydia's heart into a crueler twist. He always noticed, even when Lydia tried to hide her discomfort.

After confirming that Mother remained insulated within her circle of Lydia's potential mother-in-law candidates, the pair slipped out of the bustling ballroom and into the cool quiet of the hallway. Not unlike the last ball they'd attended together. A nagging, familiar sensation tingled in the tips of her fingers and toes.

"I always thought it was a shame you were not asked to dance more. Because I know you enjoy dancing, of course, but also because…you are a beauty to watch."

Lydia inched farther into the darkness, her back to Sebastian so he would not see the pain battling for a place on her features. For the first time in her life, she regretted allowing Sebastian to develop the intimacy to speak so sweetly to her as a form of teasing. "Thank you, Sebastian. As you know, Mother employed only the best dance tutors."

Her brows furrowed when she thought she heard a grumble buried by a cough.

"But you are the one who learned and practiced. In any case, it was a worthwhile investment. You look poised to grace the ballroom of, say, an earl."

Lydia's furrow deepened. She turned to face her friend, standing on the outskirts of the shadows, hands clasped behind his back.

"You appeared to enjoy your night at the theater."

"I did," Lydia confessed slowly. "I must say, the Season's events are a bit more enjoyable when other people at least pretend to notice you, let alone include you. I suppose I should enjoy it while it lasts before the *ton* moves on to the next spectacle."

Instead of the happiness for his friend that Lydia had expected, Sebastian's features contorted into a sour expression. It lasted a mere second, gone before Lydia's mouth could fall open and demand an explanation. She had expected Sebastian of all people to understand how long she had waited for Society's fickle favor.

"I wish you would take my word when I say that you are not a spectacle, Lydia," Sebastian insisted, his mouth a tight line.

"You are meant to say that. You are my…friend. A wonderful, selfless friend."

Sebastian took a step back, farther into the light, shaking his head. "It is the truth, and it will remain true even if I never manage to convince you otherwise," he mumbled, almost more to himself than Lydia. "But tell me more about your time at the play."

"Why?" Lydia pushed back. Why did he delay the inevitable? He need not steer her toward other gentlemen in order to free himself for Miss Woods.

"I am simply curious. We have not yet had a chance to discuss it—or these many incredible recent changes. I only hope to be a supportive friend, as you say."

"I am certainly grateful for that. Unfortunately, I have nothing terribly exciting to report. I thoroughly enjoyed the performance, of course, and Lord Kelling had a particular interest and knowledge of the actors, as drama is his dearest diversion. In fact, he spoke of almost nothing else and I now possess an appreciation for the exhaustive history and present-day intricacies of the art form."

A laugh trickled from Sebastian, echoing through the empty hallway as if he were a mile away. He looked down at his polished shoes. He had not looked Lydia in the eye since they'd quit the ballroom.

"Perhaps at your next meeting, you can share your love of Mr. Euston's art with him. Surely, an enthusiast such as himself will admire your passion."

"I am not entirely convinced I will be accepting any future invitations from Lord Kelling," Lydia confessed, a strange defensiveness pulling her shoulders back.

Sebastian shrugged. "Perhaps one of the gentlemen you danced with tonight is more to your liking? Every opportunity is before you now, Lydia. You have all the right gentlemen at your door. It is only a matter of time."

"Yes…perhaps," Lydia mumbled. If that was what he wanted to hear so badly, why did his smile waver? "What of your visit with my mother?" she demanded, unable to bear his encouragements any longer.

Those lovely, brown eyes widened. "Yes, I did visit her."

"It seems you had a rather productive conversation."

"She…clarified some matters for me," Sebastian whispered, his head hanging between broad shoulders.

Lydia ignored the wild, panicking thunder of her heart. Best to have the truth out now. She had already heard enough from Mother. She would certainly rather have the rest of it from his lips directly than hear it on a stranger's or read it in the newspaper announcements.

"And Miss Woods," she said.

"Miss Woods?"

"It is quite all right, Sebastian." Lydia took a step back, retreating just a touch. She prayed the shadows and distance would soften the undeserved hurt in her smile into the friendly happiness she had been denied.

"By all accounts, you appear to be exceedingly fond of Miss Woods," she continued. The words scraped against her raw throat as she forced them past her lips.

Lydia was not blind. She did not need anyone to tell her that Miss Woods was her exact opposite, the perfectly polite lady without all the rigidity. Mother's best attempts to create that blend in Lydia had resulted in this frigid facade, loved only by childhood friends who had glimpsed whatever warmth Mother had failed to stamp out.

"I saw the two of you dancing earlier during the first set. She looked absolutely smitten with you, and you clearly enjoy her company. A very handsome couple, indeed. Everyone who has heard the rumors says so."

"Yes," he answered after a long silence, a hint of uncertainty in his voice. "Miss Woods is indeed quite lovely."

Lydia nodded. Whatever threads had been holding her heart together came loose. "I am so very pleased for you, dear Sebastian," she lied through the hitch in her breath.

"I suppose…we were swept away by emotion that night," Sebastian whispered.

A sliver of light pooled on the wooden floor behind Sebastian, growing wider as a footman pushed it open. The cold dread of necessity seized Lydia. Picking up her skirts, she rushed through the stretch of shadow between them. They could not be seen conversing alone in the darkness, even in Lydia's own home.

She stumbled into the patch of light before Sebastian's feet just as a couple ambled through the ballroom doors, the old man's wiry, gray mutton chops twitching as he yawned. For just a breath, Sebastian's hands gripped Lydia's bare arms between the tops of her long evening gloves and the swooping ruffles of her cap sleeves. He steadied her, the inner corners of his brows angling up in a silent question Lydia could read by heart.

Nodding, Lydia hastily stepped to the side, a few more proper inches appearing between them. In truth, they should not have been alone in this hallway, just like last time, with only the occasional footman wandering back and forth to act as Lydia's chaperone. At least if they both stood in the light, they showed they had nothing to hide. Sebastian certainly did not. Lydia's heart would remain in hiding perhaps for the remainder of her days, protected from the romantic light of Sebastian and Miss Woods's bliss.

The couple waved to the young pair down the hall, their eyes bleary. "In need of fresh, cool air, eh?" the elderly gentleman asked with a wheezing chuckle. "I remember needing to do just the same all those years ago when I danced and danced and—"

"Now, now, dearest, why don't you tell me all about what you remember on the ride home?" his wife suggested, her tone slow and patient as she guided him toward the stairs. "I bid you goodnight," she offered to the observers, clearly more concerned with keeping the man on his shuffling feet than imprudent behavior. Sebastian and Lydia returned their farewells as the couple disappeared from view.

Everything carried on as usual around Lydia's fragmenting heart. The pieces had fallen together too late for her, only just.

Only just was enough of a margin when hearts were at play. Feelings were too convoluted and fleeting to waste even a moment on doubt. Lydia knew that now, a hard lesson with a singular application. She did not intend to come near such a situation ever again. Miss Woods had acted with the confidence Lydia had never quite been able to feign, washing away any influence Lady Swan's meddling may have had on Sebastian.

"I pray that tonight the only emotion to sweep you away is your love for Miss Woods," Lydia finally forced herself to say as the older couple's footsteps faded down the stairs.

"L-Love?" Sebastian sputtered, peering over his shoulders. "I do not love Miss Woods, Lydia."

"Yet," Lydia added under her breath. "She has all the qualities an intelligent, good-natured man could desire in a bride. It is only a matter of time."

Sebastian's expression went blank. Lydia seized the moment to retreat within, hot claws grazing at her stomach. She pressed a hand to her middle and hinged forward. It was easy to exaggerate an urgent and unexpected illness when she truly felt moments from betraying all sense of propriety and crumpling onto the floor right there in the hallway where half the *ton* could walk by.

"Please offer my parents my apologies, but I am afraid I am quite unwell. Overexertion, I daresay," she mumbled, fighting for every inhale.

"Heavens." Sebastian gasped quietly. His fingers reached toward Lydia. She threw a hand up between them.

"At least I am in familiar waters. I will manage on my own from here. Do not keep lovely Miss Woods waiting on my account."

Lydia did not wait for a response. Spinning on her heel, without looking back, she rushed to the stairs and stormed up. Vision blurry, she navigated the townhouse by memory.

She had lied yet again. She was not in familiar waters at all. None of Mother's training had prepared her for this. Nothing had prepared her for the ache ebbing and flowing through her chest like cresting waves, forcing her gasping head above the surface, only to drag her under again.

Discarding gloves on the floor and clumsily kicking off her ribbon-adorned slippers, Lydia collapsed on her bed. Listlessly, she tugged the diamond pins holding her curls in place. She would find a way to manage without her maid's assistance tonight. No one needed to witness the tears balancing in the corners of her eyes, forbidden from falling.

After detangling as many pins as she could reach in that position, Lydia propped herself up on one wrist, back against her ample array of pillows. Something firmer and rougher than bed linen brushed the tips of Lydia's fingers. Peering into the pillowy crevasse, she gripped a corner and pulled.

A single sheet of paper, folded in half once, no wax seal.

Lydia's heart leapt into a thundering gallop. She inhaled, bracing herself, and flipped it open.

Almost in the same breath, her heart came to a sputtering halt. This time, Lady Swan had spared only a few short words encouraging Lydia to not give up, reminding her that she was so close.

*"Your dawn shall be all the brighter for this night's darkness."*

After all the trouble she had caused Lydia, *that* was all the anonymous matchmaker had to say for herself? That must have been easy when she could hide behind quill and ink while she pulled the strings on unwilling participants' lives.

To Lydia's surprise, the elegant handwriting smudged under a dropped tear, and then another. She quickly tossed the letter away and it fluttered to the crumpled bedsheets.

Somehow, the confirmation that she had been guiding Lydia and Sebastian together all along, just as Lydia had hardly dared to hope, had opened the floodgates of her emotion. The tears streamed down her face freely now. Her chest trembled as it rose and fell with sharp, jagged breaths as she buried her face in a pillow and curled up on her side.

Her fingers crept out toward the plain sheet and dragged it closer. It had come too late. What did it matter that it was always too late? In the end, no matter how desperately Lydia had prayed these past few weeks to make up for the years she had spent ignoring her own love for Sebastian, her prayers had not been chosen for a blessing.

They would never be chosen because, no matter how delightful it had felt to finally hope and finally feel how deep love could flow, the obstacles facing a future for her and Sebastian were too great. By her very nature, Lydia could never bring happiness to Sebastian in such close quarters for so long. If anyone deserved unhindered and unbridled happiness, it was her best friend.

Foolishly, Lydia had allowed Lady Swan's influence to confuse a loving friendship for romantic compatibility. Worse yet, she had allowed it to affect Sebastian. Now there was no chance of mending, either.

What right did she have to mourn something she had not even known she'd wanted until it had been too late?

# CHAPTER EIGHTEEN

A LIGHT BREEZE tickled the back of Sebastian's neck. He swatted at his nape, irritated. The wind would obey him no more than his restless heart would. He slipped the watch from his pocket and glanced at the bridge spanning the glittering Serpentine. Every second that Miss Woods did not appear was another second Sebastian's mind could relive the disaster of the previous night.

He resumed his pacing at the foot of the bridge, hands clasped behind his back. He really had come so close to having the woman he had dreamed about his entire life…only for it all to be slowly pulled out from under him while he'd watched, confused and helpless.

His confusion had only increased since last night. He had rather expected their conversation to unfold differently. He had been bracing himself for well-deserved insults hurled at his face and tears that would scar his heart. Instead, Lydia had expected the dismantling of their brand new courtship, even steering him toward Miss Woods. Perhaps she had required assurance of his happiness with another before she could turn her favor to the lords courting her now. Sebastian was powerless to tell Lydia that his happiness was forever tied to hers—not with Mrs. Dailey's threats simmering in the back of his mind at every waking moment.

"Mr. Harrowsmith!"

Miss Woods's melodic voice drifted across the river from the opposite bank. Sebastian paused and returned the lady's bashful wave. She was the picture of spring in a cream and lavender walking dress and matching lace-trimmed bonnet, no one could deny that.

Sebastian's heart remained firmly enveloped in the depths of his stomach, where it wreaked its anxious havoc. It did not soar into the sky, floating amongst the clouds with ease like it did when Lydia entered a room.

Still, Lydia had given him her encouragement to pursue another, unasked for though it was. Her companion to the play and her partners at the ball may not have captured her affections, yet she seemed intent on taking full advantage of the unique situation she had found herself entangled in. He could hardly blame her.

Besides, everyone else saw a spark between Sebastian and Miss Woods—even Lydia. Surely, in time, he would see it, too. At the very least, he owed the lady a chance.

She wore a warm smile that complemented her round, rosy cheeks as she crested the bridge and joined Sebastian on the other side, a maid trailing behind at a respectful distance. He offered his elbow to Miss Woods and she accepted gracefully.

"Thank you for joining me today," Sebastian began, discomfort frothing in his stomach. He knew what he should do, what everyone else wanted, what made sense. Yet every fiber of his being mutinied against it even as he rehearsed the words in his head.

Miss Woods tilted her head to eye Sebastian curiously from underneath her floral bonnet. "I must confess I was surprised by the invitation."

Heat stung Sebastian's exposed skin. Had his disinterest in Miss Woods been that obvious to the lady herself? He guided them at a slow pace down the gravel path toward a shady copse. The idle symphony of birds calling and wind rustling leaves offered a welcome respite from the racket that filled Hyde Park during its bustling promenade hour.

"Is that so?" Sebastian replied with an awkward chuckle. "I hope this next part will not come as quite so much of a surprise." He paused, clearing his throat, the starched collar of his shirt painfully stiff. "After making your acquaintance last Season and spending more time with you this Season, Miss Woods, I have come to appreciate your many lovely attributes. Attributes I hope to come to know more deeply over the course of our courtship, if you would have me."

The fingers of Sebastian's free hand tapped restlessly against his leg as he spoke. The entire time, he looked straight ahead at the trees arching over the walkway. He was too embarrassed and conscious of his every movement to look Miss Woods in the eye. Not like when he was with Lydia.

He had never felt uncomfortable allowing his best friend to read the unsaid in his gaze. Except for the other night at the Daileys' ball. Lydia must never see the profound pain in his countenance.

Sebastian frowned. Forcing himself not to abandon all gentlemanly courage, he dragged his eyes away from the unfocused distance and glanced at his companion. Several breaths had passed and Miss Woods had not made any indication she had even heard Sebastian's declaration. His knees weakened at the prospect of having to repeat that flustering speech.

Just as he opened his mouth to inquire after Miss Woods's wellbeing, she halted. Sebastian stopped beside her. The lady slipped her arm out of his and turned to face him.

"I would be remiss not to confess that accepting you as a suitor would do nothing short of thrill me, Mr. Harrowsmith," Miss Woods started, a proud resignation in her eyes. "But I would also be remiss to accept you as a suitor when I know your heart belongs to another."

"If you mean Miss Dailey—"

Miss Woods lowered her face, obscured by her bonnet, and giggled. "Yes, I do mean Miss Dailey. And no matter how ardently you deny it, the truth of the matter, Mr. Harrowsmith, is that I can see your love for her written all over your features. Even now, as you continue trying to deny it."

Sebastian snapped his mouth shut, putting an abrupt end to the nonsensical sputtering bright Miss Woods had seen through. Sighing, he shook his head and rubbed his jaw. "May I ask how you…formulated that impression?"

"Well," Miss Woods said with a shrug, "I formulated it the very first instant I saw the two of you together. The night of Lady Spurgold's welcome ball. I had not yet met Miss Dailey. After the ball, I confided my interest and concerns to my friends. They reassured me that your affections had always been and would always be strictly platonic. Until last night, when my initial suspicions were confirmed."

A heavy stone of anxiety dropped onto Sebastian's chest. They could not afford to be caught in the dark again, not with Lydia's reputation already under threat from her own scheming mother.

"Do not fear, Mr. Harrowsmith." Miss Woods rested a reassuring hand on his arm. "I will not speak of it; you have my word. I bear neither you nor Miss Dailey any ill will. Finding you handsome and kind, I thought I might see if you truly were as unattached as they said. I have since discovered that your head will not be turned. Complete devotion is a trait any lady can admire."

Relief pulverized the stone to dust and Sebastian took in several deep breaths, stretching his lungs. "Thank you, Miss Woods. Truly." Sebastian lowered his head to the lady. "If it is not imprudent of me to say so, you are quite a favorite amongst several gentlemen I know. I pray one of them will prove himself worthy of your patience and good nature."

"Thank you, Mr.—"

"Mr. Harrowsmith!"

"There he is!"

Sebastian and Miss Woods whirled around to face those accusatory voices. Five of Bainbridge's boldest young ladies marched toward them, expressions somber and determined. The smattering of other park-goers peered at them curiously from beneath the shade of parasols and wide brims.

"What wonderful timing." Miss Woods laughed as the girls stopped before them, Miss Felicity Reeve leading the charge. A sixth lady, Miss Abbott's aunt and frequent chaperone, tarried by the colorful blooms lining the riverbank—within sight yet out of earshot. Sebastian's friends glanced at each other curiously. The ladies' rigid shoulders and furrowed brows softened under Miss Woods's soft, compassionate smile. "It appears I have taken the most difficult part out of your hands by voluntarily removing myself from Mr. Harrowsmith's consideration. Still, I believe he requires a bit more convincing. That, I gratefully leave to you all—and I am doubly grateful that I do not have a pack of fiercely loyal ladies chasing after me."

Miss Woods dipped into a curtsey and bid them farewell and much luck. The Bainbridge group watched her go for a silent moment, a cheery bob in her step. Smiling to himself, Sebastian promised to covertly assess the men in his circles who'd expressed jealousy over the attention Miss Woods had given him this Season and see which ones he could direct toward her.

"She is quite delightful," Miss Gardiner whispered.

"That does not matter right now, Ellen!" Miss Reeve groaned, jabbing a finger under Sebastian's nose. "Not when he is courting her!" He jerked back and offered what he hoped was a sufficiently nonchalant smile to the mildly offended passersby, as if this were a normal occurrence in his day.

"There is no need for theatrics in the middle of Hyde Park, sister," Miss Mercy snipped under her breath, grabbing her twin's arm and trying to wrest it back into place at her side as unobtrusively as possible.

"Indeed, do not waste them on me," Sebastian agreed. He took Miss Reeve's hand in both of his. "I am not, in fact, courting Miss Woods."

The younger Gardiner girl squeezed her way in between the

Reeve twins. "You are not? But your mother has been speaking of it with such certainty. Mrs. Dailey, as well, now that I think of it. Our mama said Mrs. Dailey speaks of your impending marriage to Miss Woods with as much frequency and excitement as your own mother."

Sebastian's jaw twitched. Of course Mrs. Dailey had fanned the flames of Mama's interest in Miss Woods as a daughter-in-law.

Miss Gardiner nodded, wide eyes pensive. Miss Abbott looked over her shoulder at the other lady's receding form and back to Sebastian. "If you are not courting her, then...."

"You see, I did meet with Miss Woods here with the intention of asking to court her since everyone else seemed to understand it as a certainty. But she already knew of my feelings for Lydia, having ascertained them herself through observation, and very kindly refused me."

Sebastian paused and lowered his head. "I must admit I am ashamed that I nearly took advantage of a lady's genuine feelings, and I hope to apologize to Miss Woods with all the deference she deserves as soon as possible. I should also like to thank her for helping me realize that I am in no state to court anyone, not until my feelings are well and truly resolved."

As he spoke, the ladies' features relaxed with relief and then settled into a shared knowing. "Oh, Mr. Harrowsmith, Lady Swan *did* intend for you and Lydia to make a match!" Miss Clara cried when Sebastian had finished.

"Shh!" the others hissed. Holding up a hand, Sebastian led them toward the sparse tunnel of trees for a little more privacy.

"How do you know what Lady Swan intends? Has she revealed herself?" Sebastian demanded. Intrigue sparked in him once more, mingling with the cool shadows dappling his face. He had been so lost in his own concerns recently that Lady Swan had almost entirely escaped his notice.

"No, but Lydia received a third letter. On the night of the ball," Miss Mercy explained, reciting its contents from memory in hushed tones.

"That indicates no other but you, does it not?" Miss Reeve added, giving a sharp nod of confidence, the matter entirely settled in her eyes.

"But how does she know?" Miss Abbott mused to herself.

"I am not sure I wish to discover her methods any longer," Miss Mercy replied with a shudder.

"Someone will come forth at the end of the Season, surely," chirped optimistic Miss Clara.

Sebastian cleared his throat, drawing the girls' attention. "As touched as I am to know that Lady Swan saw such potential in me, I am afraid she was mistaken."

"Pardon?" Miss Reeve demanded, not bothering to temper her scowl.

"I am not the one for Lydia."

There. Sebastian had finally said it aloud to other living souls. The cruel truth dug its claws ever deeper into Sebastian's heart, squeezing until he struggled for every beat.

"Mr. Harrowsmith, I know I speak for everyone present when I say that we consider you to be a very dear friend," Miss Abbott began, poised as if ready to deliver a lecture at Oxford. "I pray you will confide in us as friends and speak from your heart when I ask: Do you love Lydia?"

The others looked from Miss Abbott to Sebastian in awed silence. Sebastian stared back, just as surprised, though not at the frankness of the question. He had been positive that his feelings had long since been understood by his Bainbridge friends.

"Of course I do," he whispered.

*Of course.* Of course Sebastian loved Lydia. Had he not, Sebastian would not have found himself in this age-old predicament, nursing a heart that had been broken by someone who had not wanted it in the first place.

Blushes swept across every cheek. Miss Gardiner pressed her lace-covered palms to her face and burrowed behind Miss Reeve. "So romantic," Miss Clara whispered.

"Forgive me, but I thought you all knew by now," Sebastian could not help laughing despite the ever-present ache that had gnawed a home for itself in the center of his chest. He supposed this would be his first lesson in learning how to find some paltry amusement in life with that wound slicing into every breath.

"Of course we knew," Miss Reeve announced with a shrug. "But it is one thing to know it and one thing to have it confirmed."

"Especially with all of...*this* happening now," Miss Mercy continued where her sister had left off, gesturing through the air. "This Lady Swan business."

"Again, I am afraid I am not to be counted amongst Lady Swan's success stories," Sebastian insisted. "But I earnestly assure you that it matters not to me, so long as Lydia is happy. That is all that has mattered to me, always. I am sure you all were well aware of that long before now."

The ladies nodded, their expressions softening. "What makes you say that, Mr. Harrowsmith?" quiet Miss Gardiner asked, stepping forward. "Why do you say you cannot be Lady Swan's answer?"

Sebastian lowered his head. Though he appreciated their timely confidence, he was loath to repeat the vile things Mrs. Dailey had said, what she had made him promise, to any lady.

"I am not the kind of man Lydia needs. I might have been had my fortunes not changed, but it has become abundantly clear to me that I cannot give her everything she deserves."

"What about what Lydia wants?" said a quiet voice. Everyone turned to look at the youngest of the group. "I have never seen her as distraught as she was this morning when she told us of what happened at the ball and of the new letter. Do you think the misery your absence from her life causes is what she deserves?"

Sebastian's face stung as if Miss Clara had slapped him. "N-No, certainly not. But I cannot fathom why she should be distraught over me when the gentlemen who can lay the whole of London at her feet with their names alone are seeking to court her. Almost every man who has expressed interest in her since that debacle is certainly a better match than I am."

Miss Abbott sighed sharply and shook her head. "Not for Lydia, they aren't. That is what Lady Swan has been saying from the start, I am sure of it. You must know that Lydia's feelings for you have never changed, regardless of your inheritance status. She thinks the world of you." She paused. "You make her laugh," she added quietly, a touching earnestness in her voice.

Her words reverberated in Sebastian's mind. Heavens above, how he longed to be the man worthy of being Lydia's world.

Could it all come down to something that simple? He made Lydia laugh. But there was more than that under the surface. It was simple in ways he could not quite grasp.

"Has something happened, Mr. Harrowsmith?" Miss Mercy asked. She watched Sebastian with an observant gaze.

Biting the inside of his cheek, Sebastian gave up the deliberation. They were his childhood friends as well, after all. Still, he chose his words carefully as he relayed the basics of his private conversation with Lydia's mother, not wanting to shock them too terribly all at once.

Angry murmurs rippled through their little gathering, blending in with the swishing leaves above. "I never liked Mrs. Dailey," Miss Reeve spat. "I would rather have uncaring and forgetful parents like ours than suffer that miserable creature's incessant deprecation. And to threaten ruin on her own child! Poor Lydia."

Miss Mercy shuddered. "Let us hope our mother does not adopt any of Mrs. Dailey's methods. We have already had enough of a taste of motherly control this Season."

"Then you should do the brave thing and marry first." Miss Reeve elbowed her sister in the side. "Perhaps if the viscountess marries you away, she will forget about me for another few years."

"I am so sorry you had to endure such unpleasantness." Miss Gardiner's gentle voice disrupted the twins' arguing. She gave Sebastian a sympathetic smile.

"Is that why you have been urging Lydia toward her new suitors?" asked Miss Clara. "That wicked Mrs. Dailey meddled with your head!"

"Only because those insecurities already existed in my heart," Sebastian clarified with a rueful smile. "She saw what I had always feared, that I was not Lydia's equal, and confirmed it before I could steer her further astray of the golden path. Now she will forever hold that kiss over me."

Miss Abbott's chuckle drew their attention. She smiled at Sebastian like he was a child endearingly doing his best in the completely wrong way. "And here Lydia was telling us that *she* is the one who is unworthy."

Sebastian's brows furrowed. "Lydia thinks she is unworthy? How could such a thing be possible? She is the most perfect woman to have ever breathed."

"Perhaps it is time you said as much to Lydia," Miss Abbott continued. "It appears you both have been making the same assumptions about each other without knowing it. Clearly, Lady Swan, whoever and wherever she is, must have realized that unless someone stepped forth, you two would very likely miss your chance at happiness. Lydia never once mentioned her swarm of suitors this morning. She only spoke of you...and how well you look with lively Miss Woods."

Something imperceptible stirred deep in Sebastian's chest, struggling for purchase. Hope. Warm, welcome hope.

It swelled from head to foot, awakening his hibernating senses. What need did he have for senses when the woman he loved and cherished would soon be whisked away from his world, taking all color and the scent of sweet things with her?

"Do you mean to say...that Lydia does indeed share my feelings?"

The girls shot knowing glances to each other. "It is not our place to say as much," Miss Mercy began, "but should you wish to continue this conversation with Lydia, you may accompany us to Somerset House. We will be meeting with her there shortly."

The shades of shadows grew deeper. The lovely smell of spring flowers became tantalizing. Mrs. Dailey's harsh words, once looming and frightful, the verbalization of Sebastian's darkest thoughts, faded with the breeze. That was how powerful the mere hope of Lydia's love was.

"Still…" Sebastian hesitated. "That will not prevent Mrs. Dailey from keeping her word."

Miss Reeve set her mouth in a firm line. "We shall see about that."

"Please say you will come with us, Mr. Harrowsmith, please," Miss Clara begged, hands clasped under her chin. The other Bainbridge ladies watched expectantly.

Anticipation surged in Sebastian's chest. He gave his friends a single nod. As he followed them back down the path and out of Hyde Park, Lady Ainsworth dutifully trailing behind, Sebastian's mind scrambled to think of what he should say to Lydia, where to begin.

His heart hammered with a simple answer the whole way, the answer it had carried inside it his whole life.

He would just know.

# CHAPTER NINETEEN

EVEN MR. EUSTON'S artwork did nothing to lift Lydia's crushed, numb spirits. She stared up at a painting of a quaint country church dusted in snow, glistening in the beautiful gold of spring's first sunrise. It was one of Lydia's favorites. At least it had been, before everything in her life had lost meaning.

"Mrs. Dailey, there you are! May I borrow your expert eye on the color of this painting and how it would suit my drawing room?" the familiar voice of Isabel's aunt called from the next gallery over. Mother shot Lydia an unnecessary warning glance to remain where she was before quitting the exhibit. Lydia had no energy or inclination to disobey any longer. Her friends had arrived and she could hardly bring herself to care.

Sebastian could very well be marrying Miss Woods in a church just like the one in Mr. Euston's painting in a matter of weeks. Pain lanced through Lydia's heart at the thought, dispelling the unfeeling daze that often enveloped her.

It had all happened right under Lydia's nose. She had been so preoccupied with fighting the uphill battle to win Mother's love that she was blind to the love that had been freely given to her all along. Someone else had recognized the love bursting at the seams of Sebastian's soul, longing to find a home, and had done what Lydia could not—accept it.

Foolish tears stung her eyes. She lowered her face to keep them from spilling out of the corners, to prevent these magnificent works of art from witnessing her loss of control. Only when Lydia glanced about the now-empty room did she realize that it was, in fact, not empty.

"Lydia."

"Sebastian? What brings you here today? Well, the artwork, I suppose. Why else does one visit Somerset House? Did Miss Woods accompany you? And our other friends, have you seen them? They were to meet me here some time ago," Lydia blathered, unable to stop herself.

The moment her eyes landed on her best friend standing in the ornate doorway, all the pointless words that had been piling inside her surged forward. As if they had missed Sebastian and needed his presence to come to life. No one had ever muddled Lydia's mind so thoroughly that she actually babbled.

"Lydia," Sebastian repeated, the tension in his voice at odds with the flicker of hope in his eyes.

She fell silent. Her words fled. The air in the room shifted. Lydia could only stare as Sebastian took one slow step into the exhibit and then ran the remaining few, only stopping when they were toe to toe. She did not flinch or move back.

The budding ember at the center of Lydia's chest began to glow, reaching for the handsome, tender, diverting, endlessly patient man standing before her. It whispered to her to remain exactly where she was. Perhaps she had always been where she needed to be.

How she knew that Sebastian was here for her, she could not begin to guess. The rightness of that thought was absolute. She had become increasingly familiar with how wrong, how unbalanced she would feel forevermore in a world where Sebastian spent the rest of his life with another.

After a long moment of silence, tense yet not uncomfortable, Sebastian lowered his head and grasped both of Lydia's upper arms. The feeling of his warm palms on her skin as he trailed them down to her hands set her ablaze, every inch of her mind, body, and spirit tingling with promise. She itched to remove her gloves, to feel his fingers intertwined with hers.

"And here I have found you in your favorite painter's exhibit," Sebastian began. His light laugh brushed against Lydia's forehead. As strange as it seemed, she could feel his love even in his breath. "An auspicious sign, I hope." His voice, clear and close, rose above the slow crescendo of Lydia's heartbeat.

"'An auspicious sign'?" she parroted around the lump in her throat.

When Sebastian lifted his head and his eyes met Lydia's once more, she knew. She knew how she had sensed that Sebastian was here for her. Memories of their entire life together flashed through her mind.

Never had she seen Sebastian look at anyone like this. Only her.

"Firstly, I pray that you will accept my ardent, most deeply felt apologies." His fingers tightened around hers. "I never sought to hurt you, Lydia. Ever. I have been convinced for so long that I could never hope to stand beside your perfection as your equal. Especially considering your mother's overt preferences, which the circumstances of my plain name offend at every turn."

"Sebastian, if she has said something—"

A thumb brushed gentle circles against the back of Lydia's hand. He wore a familiar, patient smile, the very same one that had stolen her heart without her knowing it.

"Ultimately, my insecurities are the chief author of our present misfortunes. I did not think you would be happy with me, at least not to the fullest extent that you deserve. And the only thought more unbearable to me than my own heartache was the possibility of condemning you to anything less than absolute bliss.

"Lady Swan's letter gave me hope, but I thought it selfish to even dream that I was the one she intended for you. I acted selfishly in encouraging you to compromise your character that night at the Spurgold ball, yet I never once felt it to be a mistake until...."

Sebastian's gaze left Lydia's just long enough to glance over her shoulder at the opposite doorway, through which Mother had just disappeared.

"She did say something, then." Lydia's stomach churned. She abhorred the thought of anyone making Sebastian feel less than the incredible man he was, least of all her own mother. "Tell me."

"She initially suggested that I would learn my place once I saw your new suitors...and for added measure, she informed me that she did in fact witness our kiss and would not be above setting that information loose about London. That is the only reason I tried to encourage you to accept these new courtships. And Miss Woods herself has given us her blessing."

Lydia's mouth did not fall open in shock and disgust. Neither the threat to her reputation nor the other lady's endorsement registered in her mind. She would worry about all that later. Only one truth now remained.

"I forgive you, Sebastian. Of course I do." Lydia rushed the words out, eager to soothe his worries. "Because...."

The wild galloping in Lydia's chest slowed to a deep, steady rhythm. She slipped a hand out of Sebastian's and without hesitation rested it on his chest. Sebastian's free hand settled over hers, pressing it over his heart. The beat matched her own.

"I have only ever wanted someone to love me for who I was afraid of being. Sebastian..." Lydia paused, praying her eyes conveyed the unspeakable depth in every word. "Sebastian, you have done that all your life."

His wonderful, warm eyes glistened, hope taking root and blooming boldly.

"Now it is my turn to beg your forgiveness for taking more than twenty years to realize it." Lydia laughed, a lightness she had never experienced filling her to the very tips of her fingers.

"And for encouraging you to court Miss Woods. She seemed so suited to you. Clearly, the rest of the *ton* thinks so. In my mind, she is precisely the daughter Mother had hoped would emerge from her rigorous standards. I thought that if I had been more like her, perhaps you would have the fulfilling, cheerful future I always desired for you."

"Most precious Lydia." Sebastian sighed. "You are quite silly sometimes."

Lydia shrugged. "Only because I learned it from you."

Sebastian's head fell back, a bright laugh bursting from the depths of his chest. Lydia's heart soared into the skies with it.

"I love you, my sweet Lydia." He whispered those long-awaited words against her forehead, lips brushing over her skin.

"And I love you, my silly Sebastian." Lydia's smile spread as she spoke, savoring every letter.

"All my life, I have possessed an instinctive desire that has drawn me to you. As if I came to this Earth *for* you."

"I am so immensely grateful for that."

Sebastian rested his forehead against hers and slipped his arms around her waist. "Is this real? Or have I stumbled into one of my dreams?"

Lydia hummed thoughtfully. "I do not see why it cannot be both."

"So brilliant, so witty." He laughed into her hair.

"You make me feel like a star," she mused under her breath, tucking her face into the crook of Sebastian's neck, a peaceful weight settling over her like a down blanket. It was the most absurd thing she had ever said. She smiled into the safety of her love's embrace.

"Like that one?"

Lydia adjusted her head on Sebastian's shoulder and looked up at the faint morning star in the upper left corner of Mr. Euston's painting, shrouded in gossamer clouds. She stood straight, lips parting. Impossible. In the many times she had gazed upon this exact piece, she had never noticed that tiny light, ever present yet unseen until the right eyes found them.

A flood of tears rushed to the surface as Lydia stared in sublime wonder, smiling softly. "Do you remember what you said to me after Lady Swan's first letter arrived?"

Sebastian wrapped an arm around Lydia and pulled her into his side. He looked up at the star as well. "You will have to be more specific, my dear. I have said a great many things to you since then."

Lydia giggled, not caring that the joyful sound echoed through the small room or that her mother or even the Prince Regent himself could enter at any moment. At least Mr. Euston's waning popularity offered the benefit of an often deserted exhibit.

"You told me that I deserved my time to shine. But I realize now that I never needed it. You have always made me feel like the brightest star in the sky."

Sebastian leaned his head to one side and rested his cheek against Lydia's hair. "Now how will I ever manage to convince the brightest star in the sky to make this bumbling fool her husband?"

Heart trilling at a dizzying speed, Lydia pulled away from Sebastian, staring with wide eyes at the playful grin on his profile. She tumbled head over heels into love with her best friend all over again.

"What did you say?" she whispered, breathless and on the precipice of bursting with an elation she had never known or thought possible. She had never felt less tethered to the Earth or more alive.

Sebastian's smile turned endearingly bashful as he came toe to toe with Lydia once again. This time, he left her hands where they trembled at her sides and cupped her face. His earnest, constant gaze met hers. Time stilled. Lydia knew he could see reflected in her eyes the love and devotion that had belonged to him from the very beginning and would remain with him beyond the end.

"Allow me to try again." Sebastian chuckled, his nose brushing against hers. "Will you marry me, Lydia?"

Something wild broke free inside her. She threw her arms around Sebastian's neck and kissed him, deep and slow. Lydia forgot all else but the heavenly feeling of her beloved's lips tenderly exploring hers, savoring every moment.

This was right. It had always been right, and it always would be. That certainty pulsed steadfast and unwavering under the giddy weightlessness of a kiss even sweeter than their first.

When they finally pulled apart, Sebastian rested his chin atop Lydia's head, his arms encircling her. A perfect fit. Everything was perfect. All this time, she had been fighting for perfection when it could have been as easy as falling into Sebastian's arms. Yet as he held her now, Lydia's every regret for time wasted washed away. None of her time with Sebastian had been a waste. It had led them to this exact moment.

Sebastian finally broke the snug silence. "You know you have not actually answered me yet."

"Please forgive me." Lydia laughed lightly, gazing up into her future husband's enchanting face. "I am so utterly ecstatic that I momentarily forgot the entirety of the English language."

Sebastian raised a brow. "I only desire a single word."

The rush of elation spurred Lydia to tease her most cherished friend a little more. "Perhaps," she answered coyly.

Humor glinting in Sebastian's lovely eyes, he bent his head once more and captured Lydia's lips in another kiss.

"Has your 'perhaps' become a 'yes,' dearest Lydia?"

A true grin stretched widely across her face. "Yes, dearest Sebastian, of course I will marry you!"

SEVERAL MINUTES LATER, after a few more kisses and embraces, Lydia and Sebastian emerged arm in arm from the exhibit as the happiest engaged couple in London.

A flurry of hushed questions bombarded the pair the moment they set foot into the adjoining exhibit as their dear Bainbridge friends rushed toward them from the opposite end of the room.

Lydia and Sebastian looked at each other and laughed. Their

contented smiles and flushed faces told enough of the story. Still, Lydia had been eagerly anticipating this moment for so long—when she could finally tell her most cherished friends that she had found her perfect match. There was only one last consideration to overcome.

"Where is my mother?"

The girls exchanged glances. "Aunt Matilda saw to her," Isabel confessed. "She made it known that a countess such as herself spreading word of a lady making such terrible threats would do wonders to ruin Mrs. Dailey's reputation. It was not a pleasant exchange."

"Your mother was so distraught that she nearly ran from Somerset House." Felicity snickered. "She took your barouche, but I would wager that you already have another driver." She glanced pointedly at Sebastian.

All her worries faded into mist. For once in her life, Lydia longed to shout at the top of her lungs, to run barefoot through summer grass with reckless abandon, to laugh and laugh until her voice failed her. Sebastian's love had given her the freedom to simply feel. With him by her side, Lydia knew this elation was only the beginning.

"Yes, we are engaged!" she cheered, not the least bit concerned about the husband and wife loitering in the far corner.

"Oh, how wonderful!"

"—such a romantic setting for a proposal!"

"Of course we always knew—"

"—so very, very thrilled for you both!"

"Have you set a date for the wedding?"

The older couple offered an understanding smile of congratulations as they quietly quit the room. As the girls crushed the two sweethearts in a hug, Lydia's teary eyes followed the pair until they disappeared. They must have remembered what it was like to be happily in love with the future's promises stretching before them. She and Sebastian would be doing the very same thing decades from now, looking back on this very moment.

"Please, I beg you, release us." Sebastian wheezed out a laugh.

Air flooded Lydia's lungs again as the ladies reluctantly obeyed. "And no, Clara, we have not yet had a chance to discuss wedding day details." She chuckled fondly.

"Indeed, there will be some matters to sort first," Sebastian added with a relaxed smile. "I have already waited too long to ask this question and to receive such a perfect answer. Rest assured that obtaining Mr. Dailey's blessing is my next mission and then we will fix upon the day without delay."

"It seems Lady Swan was correct, after all," sweet Ellen said thoughtfully as the dizzying excitement settled. "The best matchmaker in the *ton*, I daresay. The letter may have been addressed to Lydia alone, but she helped two of our wonderful friends find their lifelong happiness in each other."

"If only the rest of us could write to Lady Swan." Clara sighed wistfully.

Isabel shook her head. "Not all of us desire Lady Swan's help. Or meddling, I should say."

"But how are we to know truly that this is the pairing Lady Swan intended?" Mercy wondered. "Naturally, it is the pairing we all suspected and championed, but it very well could have been a happy coincidence that her letter began this chain of events."

Lydia smiled at her oldest friend, the love of her life, her soon-to-be husband. "I know Lady Swan is correct. Sometimes the simplest truths require the most extraordinary circumstances to reveal themselves."

She was as certain of that as her love for Sebastian and his for her. She had only needed a nudge to see that life need not be so black and white, that the one she needed had been waiting for her somewhere in the middle all along.

# CHAPTER TWENTY

"Y OU THINK YOU know me well, do you?"

Sebastian narrowed his eyes and glanced at his beloved. She clung to his arm as they quit Somerset House, lifting her beautiful face to the warm, late afternoon sunlight.

"I thought so until this moment. Do not tell me! You *are* Lady Swan and this letter business was your elaborate scheme to bewitch me." Sebastian gasped dramatically as he led Lydia to his gig and helped her up.

Just yesterday the thought of driving Lydia about London in his simple gig would have only sunk him deeper into the depths of his insecurity. Today, nothing could diminish Sebastian's smile.

Lydia loved him in return. She longed to be his wife as much as he longed to be her husband. They would be driving to the nearest church this very moment if they were not required to secure Mr. Dailey's approval and wait three Sundays for the banns to be read. He climbed up after Lydia and took up the reins. Surely, he could wait another three weeks.

"No, I am most certainly not Lady Swan." Lydia laughed. Sebastian had never heard her laugh so often and so freely as she had today. She inched closer to Sebastian on the narrow seat, pressing herself against him. "In truth, after this ordeal, I am not sure I wish to know who she is. It is rather unlike me to say so, but perhaps some things are better left as mysteries."

"Some, yes, but I would rather like to know what I apparently do not know about you. And our next destination as well."

Peering up from beneath her bonnet, Lydia gave Sebastian the most mischievous look he had ever seen grace her features. "The two are related, as a matter of fact. I am of a mind to take a trip to Gunter's."

The reins fell out of Sebastian's hands. "Truly?"

"Truly."

Excitement building, Sebastian navigated them through bustling streets as quickly as possible. Mrs. Dailey had never allowed Lydia the simple pleasure of ice. When they'd been children, Sebastian would sometimes sneak her some, but as they'd grown older, Lydia had claimed that no ice flavors appealed to her. He'd known it to be a lie, another command from her mother.

When Sebastian stopped the gig under a row of shady trees opposite the famed tea shop, they sent Lydia's accompanying footman inside to fetch their treats. His hand slid over to Lydia's lap and grasped one of hers.

"Forgive me for asking once more, but are you sure we are suited?"

Lydia turned her hand in Sebastian's, threading their fingers together. When she looked at him, blue eyes as soft as the sky above, Sebastian released any lingering shadow of worry.

"Of course I am. We compensate for each other's faults and elevate each other's strengths."

Sebastian nodded, content. "An easy task for me since you are near faultless."

"'Near'?"

"You did select vanilla bean for your flavor." He shrugged, shaking his head in faux disappointment.

Lydia huffed and jutted her nose into the air. "Vanilla bean is a perfectly respectable flavor, thank you."

"Your vanilla bean, Miss Dailey. And your orange blossom, Mr. Harrowsmith." The footman distributed two frosty desserts, one in the shape of a pineapple and one in the shape of a swan.

Lydia smiled down at her elegantly carved vanilla bean bird

and took a bite. "Delicious!"

She smiled at Sebastian. His heart swelled with the joy of watching Lydia rediscover the simple pleasures in life.

"I am so gla—"

Sebastian's eyes widened as the tip of his nose went cold. Lydia giggled, smudging the dollop of ice against his skin just a bit more before pulling her hand back to cover her mouth, lace glove in her lap. It was too late. That light wheeze of laughter echoed blissfully in Sebastian's ears.

The lady's cheeks reddened and she busied herself with cleaning off Sebastian's face with a kerchief from her reticule. He snatched her wrist and pressed the back of her bare hand to his lips.

"Even after all this time, you still surprise me," he whispered. "I love you so very much."

Her embarrassed expression eased into comfort, familiarity. "I love you, too, Sebastian." Then Lydia surprised him yet again by reaching over to steal a scoop from his ice.

Sebastian grinned. He could hardly wait to experience all the ways his best friend, his wife, the one day mother of his children, would grow beside him, surprising him at every turn.

# EPILOGUE

P URE MORNING SUNLIGHT filtered down upon Bainbridge's church through wispy, languid clouds. Lydia trembled with excitement as Father led her toward the double doors. Just on the other side stood Sebastian—her husband. The word danced on the tip of her tongue, eager to be made real and everlasting.

Even from the other end of the aisle, Lydia could see the joyful tears in Sebastian's eyes as he waited for her with a smile so dazzling, it almost made her drop her father's arm and run straight to the altar.

No, Lydia decided as she stole a moment of her attention from Sebastian to take in the family, friends, and neighbors who had gathered to witness the happiest day of her life. She would savor this. She would savor every long, slow, weightless step, choosing Sebastian over and over again with each one.

When she finally came a few rows within the altar, Lydia caught the gazes of Felicity, Mercy, Isabel, Ellen, and Clara. Each had already been overcome with a range of emotions, Felicity dabbing at the corners of her mostly dry eyes while Clara quietly wept into her handkerchief. Not caring about anyone else in the room, not even Mother, who grudgingly watched the proceedings from the front pew, Lydia beamed at her friends.

She would not be here experiencing this bliss without their endless support—and that of Lady Swan, whose lack of a return address rendered delivering an invitation impossible. As Lydia and Father arrived at the altar, she wondered idly if Lady Swan was watching now, just as she had done all Season.

None of that mattered when Sebastian accepted Lydia's hand from her father. The moment had come. Sebastian's expression settled into devoted wonder. How often had Lydia seen that look and dismissed it as Sebastian being Sebastian? She would never mistake it again.

"You are absolutely beautiful," Sebastian whispered under the vicar's booming voice, thumbs brushing against her delicate lace gloves.

"As are you."

The loveliest shade of pink bloomed across Sebastian's cheeks. He smiled down at her dress, overlaid with that same blue silk net that had caught his attention in the modiste's shop. Feeling more alive than she ever had before, Lydia grinned and gave Sebastian's arm a gentle pinch. She could hardly wait to spend the rest of their lives being themselves with each other.

Laughter bubbled inside Lydia as she and Sebastian burst through the church doors and onto the lawn. She'd nearly caught her breath when an unexpected embrace squeezed it out of her. "Mrs. Harrowsmith." She gasped, eyes wide with wonder. Sebastian watched with a grin until his sister's family distracted him with hugs of their own.

"You are family now, Lydia, well and truly." The woman chuckled as she released the blushing bride and offered a trembling smile. "It would be my honor to be called 'Mother,' if you'd like. You shall always have a mother's kind affection in me. It is the least I can do to repay you for the love you have shown my son all these years, and I never realized. In fact, you were so well-suited that I took your bond entirely for granted. I pray you will forgive me for my ignorance."

"There is nothing to forgive," Lydia quickly insisted, pushing past the lump in her throat. She grasped Mrs. Harrowsmith's hands. "Of the many things I anticipate with eagerness in my new life, your parental tenderness and guidance rank highly among them."

The instant Lydia's eyes darted to her family, waiting on the grass for their turn amongst the other guests, Sebastian returned to her side and pressed a steady palm to the small of her back. She had not exchanged more than a handful of words with Mother after they had exposed her threats to Father and secured his permission to marry. The subject would remain sore for quite some time, Lydia knew, especially if the imminent arrival of Sebastian's cousin officially ended her dreams.

"May I interrupt on behalf of our nieces?" Sebastian asked. His gentle smile instantly soothed the ache that twisted Lydia's heart whenever she wondered if she and her mother would renew communication. It reminded her that she would be utterly and unabashedly happy with her new husband and her new family.

"But of course," she replied just as Dorothy and Christina came racing toward them, the breeze sweeping their giggles into the air.

"Aunt Lydia! Aunt Lydia!" the girls cheered as they skipped in a circle around the bride and groom. "Uncle Sebastian and Aunt Lydia are *married*!"

"Yes, we are," Sebastian agreed, pride brimming in his eyes as he smiled down at Lydia. She leaned into his side and released all the laughter she wanted. Indeed, she would be exceedingly happy as a member of this charming family.

After the ceremony and celebratory luncheon finished, the married couple elected to walk home arm in arm through their beloved Bainbridge. Lydia exhaled a contented sigh as she rested her head against Sebastian's shoulder for a moment.

"I pray that is the sound of all being right in your world, wife."

"Indeed it is, husband." Lydia gazed straight ahead at the long, cobbled road before them, shaded by trees that had watched them grow up together and would watch them grow old together. "I never much liked the prospect of leaving my childhood home behind when I married."

"I never much liked that prospect, either." Sebastian chuckled. He laid a hand over hers where it rested on his forearm. "Though you will still have to leave it, at least you will be able to see it from your new home—with me."

"You know, I always found Creeves Abbey to be far more comfortable and pleasant than Jenwick Park," Lydia admitted. "Perhaps because I knew you would be there. I love you, Sebastian."

"And I love you, Lydia." Her husband's tranquil sigh echoed her own. "I have imagined this moment my entire life, yet none of those wishful daydreams could have ever emulated the unspeakable joy I now feel."

Lydia's heart sang, tears welling in her eyes for the dozenth time that day. They turned onto the drive toward the home she would share with Sebastian and their children and grandchildren. Nothing had ever felt more natural, more perfect.

"Madam, one small matter. A letter has arrived for you," the butler announced, a touch perplexed, after congratulating his master and welcoming his new mistress in the foyer.

The happy couple shared a knowing glance. "Thank you, Moore."

Lydia accepted the now-familiar letter. Her heart fluttered when she read her new name, Mrs. Sebastian Harrowsmith, scrawled on the front. She turned it over to reveal a swan stamped in purple wax and wasted no time opening it as soon as the butler retreated, reading aloud.

"*Dearest Mrs. Harrowsmith, I will not keep you from your charming husband for very long—though I rather suspect he is reading this letter over your shoulder. Allow me to offer my sincerest congratulations on making a most excellent match and prayers for a fulfilling and cheerful future! Nothing brings this humble writer more joy than seeing the seeds of true love planted within a deep friendship rise to the surface and bloom.*

"*Whatever challenges face you in the future, always remember to* tend the garden of both your friendship and love. After this great test, you have discovered that the bonds you have shared from the beginning are indeed unbreakable. Thank you both for accepting a little nudge. That was all you needed. Your love accomplished the rest.

"Yours always, Lady Swan."

# About the Author

Penny Fairbanks has been a voracious reader since she could hold a book and immediately fell in love with Jane Austen and her world. Now Penny has branched out into writing her own romantic tales.

Penny lives in the Midwest with her charming husband and their aptly named cat, Prince. When she's not writing or reading, she enjoys drinking a lot of coffee and rewatching The Office.

Come follow me on Facebook to stay up to date on my latest news and coming releases.

facebook.com/pennyfairbanksauthor